D0765226

MONICA DICKENS

ENCHANTMENT

VIKING

VIKING

Published by the Penguin Group
27 Wrights Lane, London w8 5tz, England
Viking Penguin Inc., 40 West 23rd Street, New York, New York 10010, USA
Penguin Books Australia Ltd, Ringwood, Victoria, Australia
Penguin Books Canada Ltd, 2801 John Street, Markham, Ontario, Canada l3r 1b4
Penguin Books (NZ) Ltd, 182–190 Wairau Road, Auckland 10, New Zealand

Penguin Books Ltd, Registered Offices: Harmondsworth, Middlesex, England

First published 1989
1 3 5 7 9 10 8 6 4 2

Copyright © Monica Dickens 1989

All rights reserved.
Without limiting the rights under copyright
reserved above, no part of this publication may be
reproduced, stored in or introduced into a retrieval system
or transmitted, in any form or by any means (electronic, mechanical,
photocopying, recording or otherwise), without the prior
written permission of both the copyright owner and
the above publisher of this book

Printed in Great Britain by
Richard Clay Ltd, Bungay, Suffolk
Filmset in Monophoto Sabon

A CIP catalogue record for this book is available from the British Library
ISBN 0-670-82684-7

CHAPTER ONE

❧

Stealthily he prowled among the skeleton trees, sickened by the miasma of their hideous parasite growth. On either side, sharp disembodied eyes spied on him through the swaying vapours of the land of the Undead.

Ahead, the figure of the half-naked temptress beckoned.

So die, man-eating witch!

He plunged, because he tripped over a shopping-bag put down by a customer, and the draped display dummy toppled, sarong of splashily flowered acrylic sliding off her hipless form.

Tim caught her and righted her, and pulled up her shameless sarong just before Mrs Slade turned round from fingering and dithering over the rolls of patterned towelling.

'This one, do you think . . .?' She always asked Tim's advice.

'The fishes? Very nice.' Tim threw the heavy roll on to the cutting table. 'Ten metres you said?'

'Did I? I've lost the note. I hope . . .'

Mrs Slade watched anxiously while Tim measured and cut. Slash! His bold guillotine scissors decided her fate as abruptly as topping her head. Too late to recant.

'Put that Irish towelling away, young Timothy.' Mr D. coasted through the cutting counters of Fabrics and Soft Furnishings like an upright walrus in the flat waters between lunch and tea. 'It's a horrible mess here. Go and get the pins. Gail will have to re-drape that dummy.'

'I stumbled.'

'You weren't looking what you were doing,' frog-princess Lilian said.

'Naff off,' Tim told the low-slung back view of Lilian's bustling walk.

As he took aim with the poisoned dart, the sharp little eyes watched him from the rack of dotted muslin curtains.

Tim Kendall lived in a one-room flat above Brian and Jack's house, with a tiny kitchen corner and a shower and dwarf toilet, just wide enough to sit down.

He got off the bus in the wet dark and went over the busy main road, not with the small crowd waiting at the crossing lights, but darting nimbly through the slow rush-hour traffic, caught for a moment in headlights, like a crazed rabbit. Now we shall see. My brown envelope of adventure will be there, on the mat, waiting for me all day. As he hurried the hundred and fifty yards through the cold rain, he wrote an imaginary letter to the Council, telling them to move the bus stop.

The house stood right on the main road, small garden in front with dark polluted bushes and a slippery tile walk, wide bay window, past which, although the curtains were drawn, Tim crept on rubber soles to get round to his own door.

He slipped round the corner between the house and the garage, and up the outside wooden stairs with the loose step that Jack was supposed to have mended. On the platform outside his front door, behind which the brown envelope waited, he looked for the key. Panic. His keys were not in his trousers or jacket. He must have left them inside the flat. He would have to go back down and ask Brian to let him in. What would he say? He began to make up excuses.

Thank God. The keys were on the new ring with the brutish brass and leather tag clipped to his belt loop. When he took off his jacket today in the hot canteen, Gail had said, 'Why not one mauve earring, while you're at it, dear?'

❧

'He sneaks up there like a fugitive.' At the sound of the upstairs door, Cindy looked up from the books on the table. 'I don't trust him.'

'Let him alone.' Brian was getting the fire going.

'Not right, a youngster like that spends so much time alone. I can spot them at the store, you know, the loners, the quiet ones. Do their work and give no trouble, and then one day it's explosions and trouble all round, and a microphone under my nose: "He was your tenant, I understand. What are your memories of him?"' It was possible to talk and make notes at the same time. 'Oh yes, I can spot them.'

'That's right. You know. You always know.' Brian sat back and held out his hands to the obedient blaze that was bright but not yet hot.

'And you'll agree I know one day, when that runty lad comes down and slices us into small pieces. I sometimes think I should warn them about him at the store.' Cindy was in the Accounts Department at Webster's department store, where Tim worked.

'Let him alone,' Brian repeated. 'He's better than the last one we had. That scrubby girl. Perhaps you don't mind Asians in turbans padding up and down the stairs all night.'

'One Asian. One turban. I hate having lodgers. One day I'll leave.'

'Go ahead!'

'Don't raise your voice at me.' Cindy looked up at the ceiling; two floors up, they could hear Tim moving about. 'No need to let the world know our troubles.' They sometimes played a game of being a fighting married couple.

Brian got up. 'I'll start supper.'

'Suit yourself. *Have* a drink if you want.'

'I *said*, I'll start supper.' In the kitchen, Brian poured a drink, put on a plastic apron which said SKIDDAW, with a picture of that blessed mountain, and peeled potatoes cheerfully. He bought the food and planned the meals. Cindy was studying to be a chartered accountant and had to be accommodated.

3

When the fish pie was in the oven and the salad made, Brian took two whiskies through to the front-room.

'Poisson pie just about ready. Can I lay the table?'

'Not yet.' Cindy wrote furiously, stabbing at the paper, head of wavy yellow hair leaning on one hand.

'Finish afterwards.'

A shrug of the left shoulder.

'God dammit, get those bloody books off my dining-room table!'

The square right shoulder came up level with the other.

With a roar, he swept the books to the floor.

'Steady, Brian. I need this table, don't blame me.'

'Blame you – I'll kill you! Kill myself! Burn down the house! See a lawyer. Throw out your supper.'

While he scaled down the threats, Cindy got up and bent to collect the scattered books, and stood holding the pile, one leg and foot stuck out like a dancer with muscular calves, cheerful outdoors face smiling under the tumbling yellow hair, short tight skirt, spiky heels.

'Cross with Cindy, Bri?'

He laughed. He opened a bottle of wine and they had quite a matey supper. Afterwards, Cindy took a piece of hard-boiled egg out of Brian's beard, then worked at the table while he washed up and watched a nature programme. Then they went to their rooms and undressed for bed. Cindy was a man called Jack Garner, who dressed as a woman and wore a wig at home.

❧

As Tim put his key into the lock, he seemed to see through the door with X-ray eyes that IT was there. It was overdue, his adventure game entry, which would have his score at this stage, and the whole tempting set-up for his next move to extricate himself from the loathsome pit of monsters, or the forest of bones, or the clutches of the siren Witch Wey – wherever his last move had led him – in time to scuttle under the portcullis before the spikes fell, and do battle with the armoured Grots that he suspected of having bone-piercing marrow arrows set up in the guardroom.

He pushed open the door, then pulled it back and opened it again, to give it another chance. There was nothing on the mat. No square brown envelope. Nothing. The heart in him went dead. His lungs lost their elasticity. He stepped heavily on to the fibrous oatmeal carpet of his narrow studio flat and shut the door.

He changed out of his dark working suit and went to the kitchen end of the room to get a beer. He poured the beer into a pottery mug with a lid that one of his sisters had brought back from Germany. When you pressed the trigger on the handle, the pewter lid, decorated with stags' horns, did not open farther than straight upwards, which made it hard to quaff from; but it was a satisfying old Norse kind of drinking vessel that spoke of thonged leggings and foam-crested whiskers and rousting about in the Great Hall.

With the cold lid up against his cheek, Tim took a long pull, which encouraged him to get out a small frozen shepherd's pie and put it to cook in the little oven-grill on the counter. This was the time when he would have started on his next moves in the play-by-mail adventure game called *Domain of the Undead*. Tim had chosen the character of Blch, a gallant warlord, disguised as a travelling minstrel and teller of tales, whose mission was to penetrate ever deeper and deeper into the terrible treacherous land where corpses walked among the living, and the dread Captain Necrotic and his skeletal army were to be vanquished, not by brute strength and foolish courage, but only by the gambits of the swift zoetic rapier, which Blch must in the end (it might take months at this rate) discover.

Tim had stepped into these intriguing fantasy worlds through joining role-playing adventure games with two or three teenagers from the school where Brian was a teacher. They sometimes used to play round the table at Brian's house at weekends, and Tim, venturing downstairs to borrow a pair of pliers, had managed to infiltrate their game.

He was really too old for these games, of course, but they spoke to him in a language he could enjoy. He had learned quickly, and he threw himself under the skin of all kinds of bizarre characters, living the exploits and complicated predicaments they created as they went along with even more gusto than the boys.

That had been part of the trouble. Because he studied the magazines devoted to this fantastic cult, Tim knew how the games should be played, with props like blood splashes and little plastic model mutants, and legendary dialogue to match, which Neil and Gareth and Sean thought was stupid.

Tim was twenty-three and they were about sixteen. He bought new adventure programmes for them, but they never really let him into their group. When they stopped meeting round Brian's kitchen table and arranged the games at Sean's or Gareth's place (Neil's mother would not let him bring friends home), they did not invite Tim unless they needed an extra, and so he had taken up games by mail, and sod the boys.

Dozens of unseen players might be involved in each play-by-mail game. You knew about them through their role names and could send messages to them through the office of C.P. Games, who master-minded each adventure. Even if you always sent in your entry sheets promptly, the C.P. office, or the post office, usually kept you waiting for the next round. C.P. stood for Carrier Pigeon. A real bird might have been quicker. Last month, the postmen had gone in for industrial inaction just when Blch/Tim had found his way into the noxious lair of Putressa the festerwoman and was desperate to know if he had slain her, or rescued the mummy's child, or escaped with wounds that would not heal.

Anticipation of the answer added excitement to life, but the higher you let your hopes go, the deeper the let-down, as with most things in life. This evening's empty rubber mat announced that great expectations brought great disappointments.

'Expect the absolute bottom worst, then whatever you get is a bonus,' his sister Sarah had said, and she should know.

Tim opened two packets of crisps. He was very hungry. He was always hungry, but he never put on weight. He turned on the television and watched it for a while without the sound before he turned it off. He could hear Jack and Brian's voices raised from below. They didn't half go at each other sometimes, but they seemed to get on all right. One of them shouted and the other laughed. They weren't homos. Jack had a woman friend at work, and Tim had glimpsed Brian's girl friend once or twice at the house: no looker, but a great head of bright yellow hair. The men were just friends, who lived in this house together.

It would be difficult to have to cater to the moods and habits of another man. Tim was better off alone. But he was lonely. His flat was built under the roof of the house, so the side walls sloped to the ceiling, embellished by dormer windows at the front and back, with low wide sills. He sat on the front window-sill and watched the unremitting cars and vans and buses, and the people walking home to the high flats opposite, or taking out dogs, or jogging on the lighted cement paths of the little park.

If he had a dog . . . he would have to work only part time, or live with someone, or ask a neighbour to let the dog out. He would walk it in the dog-wrecked park at the side of the flats, wear a track suit, hurl sticks, throw out a matey remark to other people with dogs.

The telephone rang. He turned round quickly, as if the ring were a tap on the shoulder.

'Yes?' His sister Val said his phone-answering voice sounded as if he were in hiding. 'Oh – how are you, Mum?'

'I'm all right.' She always said that, although she could do almost nothing now without a lot of pain. 'It's how are *you*, I'm wondering about. You never ring us.'

'I haven't had any news.'

'Who wants news? I get too much of that already. Your father suspects you've had your phone cut off. So I'm ringing to prove him wrong.'

'Well done, Mum.'

'And to say I've got a lovely ham, so you must come and have a good dinner. Potatoes, corn, cauliflower cheese, sprouts. Bread and butter pudding or treacle tart?'

'Both.'

'Are you working this Saturday?'

'Let's see, er –' He had every other Saturday off. This was one of them. 'Yes, I'm afraid I am.' In the shopping centre in the maze of red brick streets behind this house, he had bumped into Gareth, buying cigarettes. Gareth's brief grunts had grudgingly indicated that they might be playing *Anarchy II* at his house. Might. Might not. It wasn't exactly an invitation, but he might not get another.

'Supper, then.' His mother's voice always sounded so light and hopeful, although she was half crippled with arthritis and married to a man known as Little Hitler to one and all at the Council offices. 'We'll have it cold.'

'What?'

'The ham.' She paused. 'Unless you've got something else planned, Tim?'

Actually I'm going out with this girl.

It was easy to lie, and pointless. The family either saw through it, or were not impressed anyway.

'No, I'd like to come.'

'Don't feel you've got to.' She was so undemanding, it killed you. 'I mean I don't want you to get like Gwen Ingles. She pops in. It's awful having to leave the door open, but I can't get up quick enough to answer the bell.

'"I'm worn out," Gwen tells Sidney, "but I'd better look in on poor Annie." And he says, "You never stop, do you Gwen, I don't know what the neighbourhood would do without you."'

Tim laughed, to show he appreciated her imitation of David Ingles mumbling over his jigsaw.

'He hates her secretly, you see.' His mother's voice speeded up with relish. She was getting into one of her sagas. 'He spends five eighths of his day plotting how to get rid of her without being

8

caught. When that case was in the papers last week about the sleeping tablets, he got the idea of keeping Gwen up late, talking and worrying her about money, and then telling her, you see, that he was worried she was having bad nights.'

'Ha ha. Oh, come on, Mum.' Ever since Tim could remember, her great indulgence had been to weave imaginary stories about people, known or unknown. As a child, he had loved it, much more than his sisters, and had joined in or even started her off.

'See that man in the field, Mum? He's going to steal milk from the cows.'

'Of course.' An eager swallow of saliva. 'Because his wife has left him with all these children and she took the money that was stuffed inside the sofa cushion . . .'

Since he grew up, it had become harder to play her game. He pretended, because it was oxygen and calories to her, especially now that her life was so limited.

'See you Saturday evening, then. Bye, Mum.'

'I love you, son.'

He turned on his radio to see whether there was a voice he knew, and walked up and down the room with it, like kids did with bigger ones in the street.

Paces the room, they would say downstairs. Back and forth like a caged lion grieving for its mate.

He sat down with the radio in his lap, and looked at it dully, while it told him about a play on in London that nobody liked. Thanks for letting me know.

The radio was much more companionable than television, where the people were in their own world and speaking to the camera, not to you. When you saw people on television, it was obvious you didn't know them, but voices you heard on the radio, you could make up faces to go with them, and imagine that you knew them.

He recognized most of the news readers, who greeted him at different times of day. He liked Mary Gordon, the Scottish girl who read news in the evening and sometimes did interviews: 'If I may just ask you this . . .', very gentle, smiling. She would have

9

soft, fleshy arms on either side of the studio microphone, rounded at the elbows.

Mary Gordon was one of the special people, men and women, that Tim collected to keep him going.

When his supper was ready at last, he heated a tin of beans – they prevented heart attacks in pigs, he had read – and poured another beer into a glass, because the German mug was too difficult when you were eating, and he was going to start working his way through a Willard Freeman book while he had his meal.

Willard Freeman was one of his current specials. He wrote brilliant solo adventure game books. This one was set in the fifteenth century, with a lot of antique period detail of clothes and food and weapons and whatever else Willard knew about, which was plenty, to catch you up in the feel of it. The reader played Varth the Vagabond, fighting and tricking his way through plagues and hooded assassins and mad monks and tidal waves and all the rest of it to reach the last secret chamber within a chamber within a chamber at the core of the giant nautilus shell, where snakes with fangs of wolves guarded the shimmering goblet of gold that would save the peasants from starvation.

Playing alone, you threw the dice to determine the character and powers of Varth, and the various magic spells and weapons that you would gain or lose as you charged and blundered through the murky medieval landscape.

The book was divided into brief numbered sections. Each gave you another set of choices: 'If you think you will reach the ruined chapel by climbing the rocks, go to 114. If you'd rather swim the river, go to 8. If you want to fight the horned beasts, go to 263.'

The trick was to try to outguess the crafty Willard, who dragged you through a maze of false clues and bewildering decisions that could block your way or finish you off, so that you had to go back to the beginning and throw the dice again for a new version of Varth.

While his shepherd's pie cooled and his mouth was full of baked beans, Tim was variously hacked to death, drowned, pushed off a precipice, stricken with the Black Death.

'Better luck next time,' commented the great Willard Freeman.

Tim finished the pie and ate an apple and a huge piece of cheese, after cutting off the green and black edges. Perhaps dying nobly for Willard was enough. He could not be bothered to keep starting the book again, but resourceful vagabond Varth, ragged and handsomely hirsute in the bold illustrations, had quite a hold on his spirit, so Tim let him cheat a bit, which a man of his rough background would do. He picked his own power numbers instead of rolling the dice, flipped through the book and marked and avoided all the sections that led to 'Bad luck!' or 'That's the end of you, chum!', won all the fights and thumping sessions illegally, and spiralled round the echoing caverns of the nautilus on his second mug of tea to slay the snakes and reach section 149: 'O valiant Varth! The Goblet of Gold is yours!'

Saviour of my oppressed people. Tim shook himself out of Varth, the rough feel and the smell of him and the strong, flat belly muscles, and apologized to Willard Freeman.

'Sorry about that.'

But Willard wouldn't mind. Everybody cheated over the game books. The quicker you got through them, the more you would buy.

It was nine thirty. On some desolate evenings, it would be too easy to crawl into the cave of sleep at a child's bedtime, so Tim had set a routine of not making his sofa into a bed until ten o'clock. Popping nuts and raisins into his mouth like a chimpanzee, he read some of the book his youngest sister Sarah had lent him. The rather ordinary person in it had a considerable sex life. Did Sarah think it would stimulate Tim into storming down to the pub to pick up a woman? Did she think it would make him feel that perhaps he too . . .?

What did it make him feel? He had not been with a girl for two years, and then it was only Kathy, and a bit of a mess, since what little they had managed to do had not been worth the chance of her husband finding out. What you haven't got, you don't miss. He certainly did not miss the worry and bother of it, and the lies. Not good lies that enhanced life, but sneaky, silly lies that women forced on you.

Love me?

Why not Thursday?

Why can't we go there? No one will see us, and George would never believe it anyway.

Of you?

Or of you. Look, Tim, if you don't want to go on with it, just say so.

In the end, Kathy had said so. That left Tim with no one. Lusty Varth the Vagabond, if there had been any sex in Willard Freeman's adventure books, could have made away with any wench he wanted. Tim couldn't.

He put Sarah's book away in a drawer, and took the cover and cushions off his sofa bed. He put on his pyjamas, and stuffed his shirt and pants into the plastic bag at the bottom of the cupboard.

He would take his washing to his mother's machine on Saturday. No, he wouldn't. The book he had bought through an advertisement in one of his adventure game magazines told him that laundrettes were likely places to pick up girls. The laundrette in the shopping centre never seemed to have anyone but run-down widowers and overburdened mothers, but you should never abandon the search, *Pocket Pickups* said. 'Try going at different times of day. Go at night if they're open late.'

In bed, he could not sleep. He lay on his back and made pictures in the narrow frame of street light on the ceiling, and worried about not being able to get up in time to allow for the buses being full. This spring, perhaps he would get a bike. Silver, with handlebars like ram's horns. *Pocket Pickups* said that a man with a bicycle was erotic. He would wear his cap back to front, and snake through the slow traffic. He would probably get killed.

He called on dreams to blot him out. He slept, but surfaced again, wide awake.

He got up. The heating was off. In the first hours after midnight, before the lorries started, Tim put out the light and sat on the

12

window-sill in the dark-blue dressing-gown that still smelled of his father, and spied on the few cars coming home from parties, late shifts, dinners, robberies, drug orgies: men and women passing below where he sat.

How did they know, driving so innocently down there on the road, that they were not passing through the sights of a rifle, resting on the sill?

CHAPTER TWO

❧

Brian and Jack were off walking in the Cotswolds on Saturday. Tim ventured down to their front door in the vain hope that his *Domain of the Undead* entry had got in with their letters, because the postman couldn't be bothered to climb the wooden steps.

Brian, in his tweed breeches with little straps and buckles below the knee, and thick socks like red drainpipes, opened the door briskly.

'No, sorry, old lad, nothing.' His beard was mixed up with the neck of his rugged sweater. 'Going to the Cotswolds,' he said stoutly, as if it were Kathmandu. 'Want to come with us?'

'On no – no thanks.' He must have asked only because he thought Tim would say no.

'Got something better to do?' Brian's eyes were like pale wet pebbles. His eyebrows, which grew upwards instead of sideways, were made of the same thick, soft hair as his beard. 'Another time, then.'

'Thanks. I mean, thanks.'

Tim would never be able to keep up with them. Even in the doorway in his socks, Brian already exuded fresh air and racing clouds and great waxed boots that were in charge of feet rather than worn by them. When he shut the door, it was as if the inside of the house were outdoors, and Tim on the porch were shut stuffily indoors.

In the afternoon, Tim went round to Gareth's house in Rydale Road that ran uphill to the modern Catholic church with a girder for a spire. The house was near the top, with a view of what was left of the old town, and the new blocks and the factory estate and the slate roofs feeding down in jumbled steps to the life-blood artery of the motorway.

Gareth opened the door, looking as if he had just got up from lying underneath his brother's van. Tim regretted his clean sweater and jeans.

Gareth, who was taller and broader than Tim, scanned him with narrowed eyes. 'We didn't think you was coming.'

'You said yesterday. You said you'd have a game this afternoon.'

'Well, we didn't think you'd come.'

The other two boys were already there, Sean tall and skinny with a raw red area round his mouth and nostrils, Neil squat and pasty, like one of the underground trolls he always brought into the games.

They were their usual uninspiring selves. Gareth was a bit sullen, biting his nails and eating crisps at the same time. To show them who was top dog, after the grudging welcome, Tim created for himself the character of a feared and fearful riot leader, sponsored by a mage. 'Like Merlin and King Arthur,' he explained to the blank faces which passed for cynicism with Gareth and Sean. Troglodyte Neil was under the table, looking for the dice. He ought to stay there.

The game was terrific. Chaos and anarchy ruled the world, as it spun dizzyingly out of sync with the galaxies, and cannoned into moons to cause avalanches and fountains of red-hot lava, like a Channel ferry restaurant-bar on a rough crossing.

Tim's character Tohubo rampaged about the stricken landscape, destroying and terrorizing with his enchanted scimitar, before which men and monsters quailed, Webster's department store toppled, Mr D. collapsed into an empty bladder, and humanoids with the faces of Tim's sister Valerie scuttled back into the yawning earthquake fissures that had spewed them.

'I am thy inescapable fate,' he told Gareth, who had put himself in the front row of the rock throwers on top of the cliff, just as he would be at a football match.

'Who . . . are . . . you?' droned Gareth, like a child reading its first book.

'The imperishable Tohubo – come down, bastardly gullion! I challenge you to a duel of wits under the Carcadian rules.'

'You what?' Neil said, and Gareth tortured his brows and fingernails in what was supposed to be thinking. It was agony, waiting for them to figure out their next moves, but they were the only adventure players Tim knew, and you couldn't exactly go up to people in the street and say, 'I know this fascinating way of spending two or three hours.'

'I bloody well drop this bloody rock on top of you,' Gareth chanted, 'an' then, while your stupid head's pinned down and squashed, I chop you with that axe I got.'

'Can't do that.' Sean was referee. 'You lost all your weapon points.'

'Who says? I still gotta axe and a long butcher's knife.'

'The rules say.'

'Sod the rules. I dismembered him.' Gareth was into hack and slash. It was the only way he knew to play the game.

'Perfidious swine!' Tim was enjoying himself too much to be wiped out. 'My spirit is unquelled!'

He saw himself, standing, head thrown back and legs apart, hurling a challenge at the sheer cliff, and all the voices of the great heroic ages rushing past him on the howling wind.

'My magnetic field deflects your paltry rock, and I will live to see thee damned!'

'Knock it off, for Christ's sake.' Gareth and Sean rolled their eyes. Neil was trying to puzzle out what he was supposed to be doing.

Gareth's older brother, in full black leather, opened the door, said, 'Jesus!' and slammed out again.

Tim felt great, but the boys were fed up with him. They argued grumpily about whether Tim was dead or not, and when he proved by points that he still survived, Gareth said, 'I've had enough of it anyway. Stupid kid's game,' and leaned his powerful torso over the table and messed up the papers, and the little dwarfs and gnomes that Neil had scattered about.

16

'Why can't we –' Tim asked, as himself. As Tohubo, he would have been able to declare, 'We'll finish!'

'Since you ask,' Gareth said obligingly, 'because you spoiled it.'

He jerked his chin at Tim and stuck out his lower lip. 'You're weird, you know. When I'm twenty-three, I won't be doing this kind of stuff.'

'No – you'll be out hacking real people,' Tim said brilliantly, and left.

Outside the front door, Gareth's brother was doing something to the engine of his van. He straightened up and stared Tim out of the gate. Tim turned right and walked casually for a few yards, squaring his shoulders under Tohubo's invincible armour, then sneaked a look back to see Gareth's brother bent over the van again, and ran off down the hill.

It was too early to go to Rawley, where his parents lived. If he got there while it was still light, his father would expect him to go out to the workshop shed and hold the end of something, or sand a bit of boring wood. Tim went into the town and weaved his way through the shopping precinct, where women with double push-chairs charged him like charioteers, to the cathedral. It was a fairly famous Norman pile which attracted quite a few visitors, but not in the cold weather. It was almost as cold inside as out, because there were not enough winter visitors to justify heating it properly.

Pocket Pickups did not list cathedrals as places to meet girls. Tim made his traditional tour, with his hands in his pockets because he had left his gloves at home. Up the left side, behind the altar where the wedge-shaped chapels were fitted into the apse like pieces of cold pie, down the other aisle, to look into the ornate cage where Sir Leonard and his stone lady lay, side by side, both raised on one elbow as if they were expecting breakfast in bed. Then a side trip to the north-door transept, since it was not fair to come in here without at least acknowledging the eternal presence of the suffering Christ, waiting for the world to straighten itself out, so that He could come down from the cross and go about His business.

Tim sat down on the narrow bench opposite the mysterious figure, and relaxed the guard that he had put up against the knowledge of having made an idiot of himself at Gareth's house. Weird, Gareth had said, with mean eyes, his fat, wet lip sucking what he thought was a moustache. But Tim was right and they were wrong. They were the idiots. Trouble was, they didn't know it.

It was a very old and treasured crucifix: the wood paled to silver-grey and intriguingly worm-eaten, the mournful tilted face pitted like acne, the sad folds of the loincloth. He was always draped, on any crucifix. You could never see what He had. Did He suffer that little problem too, along with all his other burdens?

Tim spread his arms along the back of the bench, straightened out his legs and crossed his feet. He dropped his head and tried to feel the flaming agony of the wounds, the thrust of rusty nails through skin and flesh and ligament, crushing bone, and the dead weight of his body hanging there.

Footsteps came down the aisle behind him. He straightened up and put his hands in his lap, rubbing his palms to convince himself that he had felt the wounds. Two women walked past the end of the bench. One of them stopped and looked up at the crucifix, and the scarred wooden eyes looked blankly down at her. If Tim were up there on the cross, his living eyes would meet the woman's upturned face, and she would nod to herself: Yes, that's him.

She lowered her head. Turn it to the right, then, away from the pitted corpse, and see on the bench the living man. If he held out his hands and blood dripped from them, would she kneel in tears before the stigmata? She walked on after the other woman.

Tim got up and went to the back of the cathedral and out of the low exit beside the main door. Still a bit early, so he went into a coffee bar.

'See the stunning blonde at the counter?' In the world of *Pocket Pickups*, girls on their own were always stunning or smashing, although if they really were, they wouldn't be alone. 'The stool next to her is empty. Sit on it. Order what you want confidently (cappuccino is classy). Ask her to pass the sugar.'

There were no stools at the counter. Tim took his tea and Bath bun to an empty table. 'She is sitting alone at a table for two. Ask her if she's waiting for someone. If it's no, you say, "Mind if I . . ." and sit opposite her. If she doesn't look up, say something, anything, ask her about the book she's reading.' *Pocket Pickups* girls were always reading. Real girls were not, but if they were, it would take more nerve than Tim had to interrupt.

Read any good books lately? Read *Pocket Pickups*?

More people came in, and an elderly man with a wobbly mauve lump on his cheek brought his cup of tea to Tim's table, slopping it over the biscuits in the saucer. Tim went to the counter and got him some more biscuits, the sort of gesture the man would not forget.

I met this delightful young man in the Coffeepot. Best sort of type. Pity they aren't all like that.

Fetching the biscuits gave Tim the licence to talk. Because the man saw him as helpful, Tim told him that he was a psychiatric nurse in a London hospital, and elaborated briefly on the work and the dedication involved.

'I admire that,' the man said. 'Couldn't do it myself, but it takes all kinds.'

Tim felt restored. He forgot the eye-rolling and carping of Gareth and Sean, and remembered only the exhilaration of being Tohubo. It was like picking one coin up from a counter and leaving another behind. This was the great trick to life. He had the secret of the universe, if anyone cared to learn. Select your own memories. Throw away what hurts.

His mother was in the kitchen, waddling pluckily about among the preparations for one of her enormous meals. Her knees had become silted up with arthritis, but her arms and hands were fully functioning. She stumped the awkward distances between stove and sink and refrigerator with her knees straight and her legs rather wide apart, like artificial ones, mashing potato and slicing vegetables and making rich gravy as zestfully as she had done all Tim's life.

19

Tim's sister Sarah was in the house, but she was up in her room, so he sat at the kitchen table with a beer, because his mother would not let him help. He told her about his week, with a few added attractions to stop her saying, 'I worry about you,' and she told him one of her tall tales about a deliveryman who she imagined was a disgraced financier.

Tim was happy to let it wash over him, but he could not be bothered to join in with her speculations about whether the man had escaped from prison and stolen the van, or was working to atone. When Tim was a child with no sense of himself, he had shared all this with her eagerly. Now her endless romances about other people were boring and irrelevant. Let people invent their own dramas and dreams. The true romances were only about the self.

The back door opened wide on the cold evening air, and remained open while Tim's father bent over on the step and coughed as if he had swallowed a hedgehog.

'Come in and shut the door,' his wife said.

❧

No one sympathized with Wallace's cough, since he was not prepared to give up smoking just to please his family and the doctor. No one told Wallace Kendall what to do. In his powerful days as Clerk of the Works for the Town Council, he had told everybody else what to do. Why should he change with retirement?

He came into the kitchen and banged the door hard enough to bring one of Annie's silly little texts off its nail. KISS THE COOK. It lay on the floor and he stepped over it.

His son, the son he had wanted born first, not last, and strong and manly instead of – well, his size was not his fault, but other things were – was lolling at the table while his poor mother did all the work.

''Lo, Father.' It was a current affectation among Wallace's children to call him Father in a derisive way, as if he were something the cat had dragged in. 'How's it going?'

Before Timothy had even finished the question, he had obviously stopped listening.

'I finished two salad bowls, if you're interested.' Wallace stood looking down at the irritating top of Tim's small head. 'Why didn't you come earlier? I wanted you to do a bit of hand sanding for me. Was that too much to ask?'

'You shouldn't have stayed out so long, Wallace,' Annie said, in the comfortable way she tried to soothe people down if she could see they were a bit upset. 'It's getting dark.'

'I couldn't see a bloody thing. Nearly cut my finger off, if you want to know.'

'Oh dear, let's see.'

You could come in with half your thumb hanging off, and she'd still coo at you as if you were a two-year-old with a scratched knee.

'It's all *right*.' He snatched away his hand. 'No thanks to working with sharp tools in that bad light, waiting for this young man.'

'His name is Tim,' his wife reminded him, 'and he's only just got back from working hard all day.'

Implying her husband had done nothing. But I've worked more Saturdays than my children have had hot dinners, and that's saying something with this mother who buys love with food. Out all weathers on the housing sites. Mud and clay up over your boots, from cutting the first sod to tightening the last door handle. Everything that went wrong was always my fault, and I'd to answer for it. Floods, electrical blow-outs, poor workmanship, the lot.

'Just back from work?' he tapped the back of Tim's head with the handle of his penknife. 'You go to the shop in jeans these days?'

'I went home to change.'

'Must have clocked off early.'

'One of us always gets off early, Fridays and Saturdays.'

'How was it?' Wallace did not sit down. He needed the height over his son.

'How was what?' When he looks up at you with those wool-gathering eyes, and his ears and adam's apple sticking out, you wonder whether your genes went astray.

'Work, of course. Or don't they call it work, nancying about with satin and scissors?'

'It was all right.'

'Was it, though? Funny thing. I was in Webster's this morning.'

'I thought you went to the library,' Annie said.

'I did, and when I'd looked up the Victorian napkin-ring design, I went on to pick up some socks, at Webster's robbery prices. Walked right through the stuffy stuff department, for a laugh, and never saw my son.'

The subject blushed like an August dahlia. 'I was on my coffee break.'

'How do you know? I've not said what time I was there.'

'Well, he must have been,' Annie said, turning round from the oven – and she could hold her own in the red flush stakes too, but of course you were going to get that, at her age – 'else you'd have seen him.'

'I don't believe he was at work.' Something prompted Wallace Kendall to say that, although it could not have mattered less, one way or the other.

Tim got up. '*I* don't believe you were in the store.'

'Now, boys, you're being very silly.' Annie moved to stand between them, but she had to put down a saucepan first, and then it took her so long to come across the room that her husband had moved away to the back hall, and was stepping out of his overalls. He put his hand in the pocket of the old working jacket that he used to wear on site. It was on a hook under Tim's anorak. (The boy always had to hang his coat on top of yours, just to annoy you, when there were hooks free.) He took out the new lipstick that he had picked up from the floor of the car after Sarah had taken it shopping.

'While I was in Webster's,' he said loftily, 'I bought a little present for m'wife.'

She was thrilled, poor woman. She smeared it on in the mirror that she had put up behind the larder door, because if someone was at the door, she couldn't run upstairs.

Tim tried to say, 'We don't sell that – that – that brand.'

22

'How do you know? If you're doing such a slap-up job in Fabrics as you claim, what are you doing mooning about in the Cosmetics Department?' Timothy was standing on the painted stool, getting something off a top shelf for his mother. 'Looking at girls?' Wallace gave him a jab in the waist with his strong craftsman's forefinger.

❧

Sarah asked, 'New lipstick, Mum?'

'Ye-e-es.' Annie spread her full lips, now much too bright a red. 'Like it?'

'It's a change from your pink.'

'Your father gave it to me.' She brought the new lipstick out of her apron pocket.

Mine. 'Where did you get that, Father?'

'In Webster's.' Sarah's father gave Tim an ugly sly look. What was he up to? Tim, drinking sherry by the sitting-room fire, turned away and put the glass on the mantelpiece.

Leave Timmy alone. Sarah often wanted to pummel her father. In the past sometimes she had.

'Wasn't it nice of him?' Whatever was going on, Annie was unaware of it.

'If you decide it's the wrong colour for you, Mum – no, don't get insecure, I'm not saying it *is* – let me have it. It's the same as the new one I bought the other day. And lost.'

Sarah looked at her father, but he had lit a cigarette and was bent double in the armchair, coughing.

'Hot cooked celery is an aprodaysiac,' Tim said, boldly for him.

'Aphrodisiac.' Valerie leaned forward and gave him her stare, framed in glasses with dark square tops, like eyebrows. She ran a play school for handicapped children, and went with a fellow who was working for a degree in psychology, so of course she knew.

23

'How do you know?' Sarah asked Tim.

'I read it somewhere.'

'Where?'

'Oh, somewhere.' Tim always went vague if you pinned him down, even if he had the answer, so you never knew if he was telling the truth or not.

'In that book I lent you – *London Lechery*?'

Sarah's father put down his knife and fork to pronounce, but he was hungry, so he picked them up again.

'I don't know. It said that the celery' – Tim took up a limp length on his fork – 'gives off these sort of pharaoh . . . chemical whatnots. Like dogs and insects, when they – they're in the mood.'

'Better not have any, then, Sarah,' Wallace Kendall bantered, with amazing wit. Perhaps there was hope for Little Hitler yet.

'I told you, the name is Zara.'

'Oh, that.'

'Yes, that. If you don't want me to call you Wally, you can remember my name is now Zara.'

Sarah had been in trouble in the last few years. After she had finally left the bastard she was living with and been through treatment to get herself off drugs and alcohol, she had announced, 'A new me, name and everything. I don't want anything of the old one.'

Perhaps Wally was mellowing towards her because she was going to a friend in Australia for several months. She could go to pot Down Under to her heart's content, and he would not have to know about it.

❦

Tim did not want her to go. Sarah-Zara was the sister he needed. Valerie, 'the clever one', had always been a witch to him. Even after she cut her stringy black hair and had wires pulled round her teeth to make her look less like a vampire, Val had always made him uneasy with her stares and criticisms and general air of knowing more and liking less about him than he did himself.

'You still content with your little bed-sitter?' she asked him after supper.

'It's a flat,' he said, 'a studio flat.'

'And you're an artist. It's a dingy bed-sitter. One of these days, I'm going to come up there with a pot of paint and do up those khaki walls in frosted white.'

'I like it how it is.'

'No, you don't, it needs brightening up. Colin and I have been helping Helen Brown to do up her place. It's done wonders for her.'

'What's wrong with her?' Zara asked suspiciously.

'Nothing. She's a bit lonely, like a lot of separated women who think they want freedom, but then can't use it.'

'So Tim ought to meet her,' Zara said. Val was always trying to fix him up with her stray dogs.

'Why not? He can't go on like this, not having any girl friends. He's getting very introverted.'

'Leave him alone.' Zara, who Tim ought to have protected from all the evils that assaulted her, was always the one who defended him. 'Don't talk about my Timmy as if he wasn't there.'

'Well, half the time he isn't. I'll ask Helen round some time, Tim, and you can just happen to drop in.'

'Oh, I don't know, Val . . .'

'Got sisters?' *Pocket Pickups* asked. 'Use them. Statistics show that 1.5 men out of 4 make exciting relationships with girls who were introduced by their sisters.'

'You go, Tim,' his mother said. 'I've met Helen once, with Val. Her husband was in the merchant navy, wasn't he? Perhaps she needs you.' Her eyes brightened to a saga. 'She's been badly hurt by this dreadful drunken sailor and needs a white knight to rescue her. She sits alone' – the relishing intake of breath – 'alone at the window of her poor basement flat –'

'Go it, Mum, she's on the fourth floor,' from Val.

'Looking up to the sunlight and wishing she could live again. I daresay,' Annie invented, 'the poor soul cares for a crabby widowed mother, but there are dozens of perfectly comfortable nursing-homes about, I don't know why people make such a fuss.'

Before he went home, Tim put his arms round his skinny younger sister, and hugged her.

'I wish you weren't going away, Zara.' He always remembered to call her that.

Zara pushed back her front hair. She had thick curly hair that hung forward, so that she could push it back, and let it fall over her face again.

Holding her hair, she scanned his face alertly. 'Shall we have a cry?'

He shook his head and looked away.

'Tell you what,' Zara said, 'if you can pay the registration and insurance, I might let you use my car while I'm gone.'

'Your car!' Tim pulled away from her. He wanted to prance about hooting, with his knees up.

'So much for brotherly love.' His father came into the hall from the basement stairs, where he had been listening. 'Won't miss her now, will he? If he's expecting to swank about in that little yellow rust-bucket, he'll be scared to death that mongrel drug pusher from Barbados will come sniffing round again (hot celery, eh?) and persuade her not to leave.'

Zara threw a punch at him, and he caught her wrist and held her off while she tried to kick at his legs with a bare foot.

Her mother said, 'Wallace – really!' and laughed. Relentlessly thinking the best of everybody, she took him with a grain of salt, and believed everybody else did too.

She had never really rumbled Little Hitler.

Brian and Jack had gone to bed, but Tim still slunk past their front bay window like a marauding cat. He sprang up his own outside stairs like the lean runner going up those endless steps in white socks to touch the Olympic torch into flame, with the whole world watching, and fell into his nest, his cave, his dun-brown burrow.

It was on the table. The envelope from C.P. Games with his play-by-mail entry forms, and a note from Brian on a scrap from the waste-paper basket.

'Sorry. Found this in with ours.'

He had been up here. What had Tim left lying about? He took a quick look round. Nothing private.

Sunday tomorrow. Tim could sleep late. With an expectant sigh, he opened the envelope and settled down to steer cunning, persuasive Blch, silver-tongued story-teller with a despot's heart of steel, through the perils and pitfalls of *Domain of the Undead*.

CHAPTER THREE

❧

After two or three weeks, Valerie did ring him about Helen Brown. Val and Colin had tickets for a musical show at the new theatre in the town, and the friends who were booked with them could not go. She had invited Helen. Would Tim like the other ticket?

'I don't know, Val,' he said. 'I'll have to look at my calendar.'

'Come on, Tim,' she said, as if she knew he hadn't got one. 'You know you love the theatre.' He did. In the summer he was going to volunteer again at the Boathouse, the little repertory theatre down by the river.

'All right, then.' At least it was a musical. If he had to sit by this Helen person, he would be wrapped round in music and not have to make conversation.

She was not much in the talk line herself. They all had pizzas before the show. Helen Brown sat across the table and hardly looked at Tim. She ate her pizza slowly, with sticky cheese on her narrow chin, and listened to Colin holding forth. She was short, which was just as well, quite a lot shorter than Tim.

Helen had unassuming biscuit-coloured hair held back with a stringy bit of ribbon, not smart, by Webster's haberdashery standards, but better than the great harsh-toothed clips the girls stuck in their heads, which they might whip off in a flash and use to crush your knuckles.

Tim thought she was older than he was, and she had been through this marriage to the drunken sailor, and the turbulent shoals of a separation or a divorce, but it did not show on her. She was not your experienced divorcee. Nor was she your hapless maiden yearning to be rescued by a white knight. She was quite old-looking, to tell the truth, and quite ugly. Bits that should be big, like eyes and mouth and bosoms, were small, and bits that should be small were big.

At the theatre, Val told Helen to go down the row first, and Tim hung back, hoping that Colin would go next, then his sister, then him, on the aisle. But Val pushed him in next to Helen, and then went to the bar with Colin. Helen did not want to go, so Tim stayed. They had to wait in their seats for quite a time, getting up to let people through who had timed it better. After they read their programmes, he had to say something.

'Have you known my – Val – my sister long?'

'I used to see her quite a lot. I had a little boy in her play school.'

'Oh?' Most of Valerie's customers were screwed up, above or below the neck.

'He's in boarding school now.'

'Oh.' He must have grown out of it, whatever it was.

She had spoken without turning her head, looking towards the stage where the curtain waited to reveal delights, quivering slightly at the bottom, a bulge appearing here and there at elbow or buttocks height, like the stomach of a pregnant woman.

'So you live – I mean, you're on your own.' Keep calm, I'm not a rapist. I just sound like that.

'When I'm at home. I'm employed at the Hall School.' A teacher? She did not look or sound like one. 'Do you know it? I'm in the housekeeping department.'

'That's nice.'

'Fair.' She made a face that did not improve the shape of her nose and mouth. 'It leaves me free weekends and holidays when Julian comes home.'

Well done, Tim. 'Ask her to tell you about herself' (*Pocket Pickups*). 'No girl can resist that. She'll think you're sensitive and understanding.'

She'll tell you a few boring things and then shut up and read her programme again. Val and Colin had come back from the bar, but were talking earnestly together, in the way they did. Now Helen should be asking Tim about himself.

She didn't, so he cleared his throat. 'I work at Webster's. I expect you know it.'

'Yes.'

'I'm in Fabrics and Soft Furnishings. It's a –' It's a what? A drag, a fine store, a bore, a challenge, nest of thieves?

She waited, the flattish front of her grey-pink jumper going mildly up and down as her narrow ribs breathed.

Two women in black ducked through a hole under the front of the stage. Thank God, the orchestra was coming in. Young men, grey men, competent girls, old bags with cellos. Tim and Helen watched while they tuned up in that wonderful carefree discordance, and then the conductor came out of the hole and summoned a crash of sound, and the disembodied voices started and the curtain went up, and Tim's senses were invaded by swirls of colour and sound.

Once, when he looked down, he was quite surprised to see the reality of Helen's grey wool lap beside him, her hands lying together like dead leaves. He looked at her to see if she was enjoying the show. She wasn't looking at the stage. She was looking at him.

Help! Did he look ridiculous, carried away like that? But she was not laughing at him. She looked rather glum.

The package from C.P. Games revealed that *Domain of the Undead* had progressed quite a bit since Tim last sent in his movement sheets. The ploys of his disguised warlord character Blch, to infiltrate behind the desecrated graves and burst coffins which were the front lines of Necrotic's ghoulish army, had succeeded, but so had the slaughter waged by giant maggots on the churls who kept the Pass of Perish.

'Your back-up party now has only a dozen plus-2 weapons and three mage spells,' said the message from Kevin Sills, who ran the C.P. office end of this game. 'It has been said that men with heads of beasts have been seen in the dead oak forest behind you. In the mountain hexes ahead, those whose super power points have not doubled will not get through, or die trying to.'

Using the map, Tim now had to find a way round the heaving bog, or go underground through the catacombs, where booby traps of foetid gases could turn you into a dybbuk and you would have to pay another five pounds to start the game again.

Some characters had disappeared, as other players got sick of them, or were killed off, or dybbuked, or ran out of money. Some new characters had turned up, to complicate the struggle for conquest, and Captain Necrotic seemed to have played a dirty trick by metamorphosing into the living human form of the Black Monk, once trusted by the people, but now a diabolic traitor.

Tim wrote a note to Monk, care of C.P. Games, protesting, 'Not Fair!', because some of the disguised Blch's possessions had been entrusted to the Black Monk's care. 'Now I don't know if I've still got 'em. What are you playing at?'

He also wrote to whoever was playing Grue, to discuss some technical matters connected with the poisoned-draught capacity of a mummy's skull. Grue did not reply – probably an illiterate twelve-year-old – but Necrotic, alias Black Monk, wrote back fairly soon: 'Wot am I playing at? I'm playing the game, aren't U? My name is DeAth. Trust me.' That could mean 'Don't trust me' in fantasy game strategy.

Tim wrote back. Necrotic's name was H. V. Trotman, and the address at the top of his small, cramped postcard was – amazing! The forces of fate were at work – a small town only about ten miles away.

'We might run into each other some time,' Tim wrote. 'Who knows?' It would be interesting to discuss fantasy affairs, and, with any luck, H. V. Trotman might turn out to have a decent games group, more reasonable than Gareth and Co.

Fired up by letter writing, Tim bought a new pad of paper and a green Biro in Webster's Stationery at employees' discount, and risked a letter to the BBC to Mary Gordon, who, though obviously not over the hill, sometimes captured hints of his mother's comfortable reassurances, as when she promised him 'alovely (she always said it as one word) sunny day'. He wanted to write to her, 'You are the sister I would like to have.'

He wrote carefully, with some curlicues on the capital letters to please her eye. 'May I ask for a picture of yourself? I enclose stamps.'

This was his lucky month, this chill and windswept March, when the cold blasted you outside Webster's staff entrance, howling down the alley, and even Mary Gordon could not promise lovely days. She sent him a photograph with a printed signature. It was amazing. She did look like someone's sister, with undemanding hair and a smile that turned up more at one side than the other.

It was quite a little picture. Poor Mary. She was probably being exploited on a small salary. Tim put it in his wallet, but took it out the next day in case he was run over in the street, and put it into the drawer with his fantasy books and games material. The drawer was locked, in case Brian or Jack came up to the flat.

Brian did come up one evening when Tim was working through a Willard Freeman book in his pyjamas and navy dressing-gown. He had the grace to knock instead of using his key, so Tim had time to put the book and dice and bowl of sugared popcorn away. Was there time to put his clothes back on? A second knock and a friendly shout sent him to open the door.

Brian had a piece of treacle tart on a plate.

'This was so good, we thought you should have some.'

'Thanks – I mean, thanks, it's –'

Must he invite him in? Brian did not look surprised at the dressing-gown and pyjama legs, but he did raise an eyebrow and say, 'Bit cold for bare feet,' before he turned and went nippily down the outside staircase with his knees turned out.

Tim's feet were long and pale, with good straight toes, because his mother had heard of children whose toes had been deformed by ill-fitting shoes, and even of a mythical character who had developed a club foot from wearing shrunken socks.

Tim guessed and cheated his way to the end of *Abominable*

Pestman: Another Fantastic Freeman Fantasy. Caught up in the adventure, he could not bother with all the rules. If he learned that leeches had sucked out every last drop of his body fluids, or that his limbs had been torn off his torso by two mastodons galloping in different directions, he resuscitated himself with an illegal roll of the dice. Back among the devilish intrigues of Willard's mind and his intricate baroque illustrations, Tim achieved, with a muffled shout, the paragraph that cried, 'Marvellous you! Abominable One is vanquished, and Our Hero lives to triumph again in another Fantastic Freeman Fantasy (see inside back cover for titles).'

Closing the book with a sigh, Tim got out the pad and green Biro, and wrote to Willard Freeman, at the publisher's address, for a photograph. He would start a collection. People did this. They stuck the pictures in albums that were sold for thousands of pounds after their death.

A few days after he had gone to the theatre with Helen Brown, a letter from the great Willard Freeman was on the doormat when he came home from work. Tim was hardly surprised. Luck came in peaks and chasms, and his was soaring. There was no photograph. 'A pic? No, you don't catch me, mate. I stalk among mankind unknown.' The letter was short and breezy and Tim folded it carefully and carried it to work next day in his inside jacket pocket.

'Good luck, chum,' it ended. 'All the best, Bill.' Hospital staff would be quite impressed to read that, if Tim was run over.

The potency of it sent him up the stairs to the second floor at a run, instead of leaning against the wall of the lift, and carried him lightly over the heavy duty carpet, as he approached the department office by his traditional route of marching and countermarching between the rows of cutting tables, slapping their cool formica tops to a military rhythm.

'Take off that face,' Fred said. 'It's only Tuesday.'

'My good news day.' Tim grinned.

Fred grumbled at him, as they went into the office for Mr D. to inspect them: hair, shave, and the clothes brush handed silently for application to The Suit.

33

'Good luck, chum. All the best.'

The folded letter in Tim's pocket kept him happy and untroubled through the morning. When his lunch hour came, he took a piece of paper and an envelope and a stamp from Mr D.'s office, and wrote another fan letter to Willard Freeman while he was eating sausages in the canteen.

'Ever your faithful admirer, Tim W. Kendall.'

After posting it in the street outside, he went up in the lift, and traversed the second floor enigmatically, easing himself round display racks and draped dummies and turgid customers: invisible man. 'I stalk among mankind unseen.'

By the end of the afternoon, the pleasures of hero-worship and daydreams had begun to seep away like a rain puddle soaking into the earth. It was always like this. The waters of fantasy ebbed and flowed. Sometimes he was quite fanatically absorbed, and then the whole thing would start to seem silly and childish, and he bundled all the games and books into the drawer, and was bored and lonely again.

Back in the flat, he opened a tin and ate a whole steamed pudding, cold, because he was too hungry to wait for it to heat up, and lay on the floor to digest it and examine his life.

Where are you going?

Last summer, they had done *Godspell* at the Boathouse Theatre. 'Where are you going? Where are you going? Can you take me with you? For my hand is cold and needs warmth. Where are you going?'

He was good enough at his job to be department manager one day, but Mr D. would not retire for ten or fifteen years. The best Tim could hope for was that Lilian got pregnant, and Tim could spend six months or so in her place as assistant manager, with a larger plastic label to accommodate name and rank.

Why would Tim, the youngest, be chosen over Gail or Fred? Because Gail was a rebellious girl who threatened every week to drop out and pursue her real career in fashion design, and Fred was getting past it, to say the least. He knew his fabrics, and could add up and multiply to make your head reel, without using a calculator, but his lips and teeth were slack, and over the backs of his hands, very evident in this line of work (Tim's were too small, but you could call them deft and artistic), crawled knotty veins and scaly patches.

🍂

'Our boy is dangerously quiet this evening,' Brian said to Cindy. 'I haven't heard the radio or the telly since he came in, and none of that condemned cell pacing.'

'I hope he hasn't overdosed.' Cindy was stretched out in the most comfortable armchair, wiggling her large toes and liking the feel of her 10-denier tights. 'I'm afraid he's rather lonely. Do you think we should invite him down here, or take him out for a meal?'

'With you dressed like that?'

'Why not? I pass, don't I – arms shaved and tits level?'

'Now listen, Jack.' Brian was getting angry; his eyes narrowed and almost disappeared. 'When we bought this house together, you swore you'd never take any chances outside. Enough's enough.'

'For you, it is. What about me? Why can't I go public? Cross-dressing's not illegal.'

'Unless someone spots you and complains. Then you're up for Conduct Leading to Breach of the Peace.'

'I'm going out for a walk tonight.'

'And get killed by the local rapist.'

Jack sighed. 'It's always the woman that pays.'

'You want a divorce?' They were off into their game. 'I get the house, though, remember that. You can have the children.'

'What would the children say?'

'Ask them.'

'We never had any.'

'That's what's been wrong with our marriage from the start.'

'And who's at fault?' Cindy sat up and pointed a finger with a carved jadeite ring on it.

'You.'

'You, Bri. My sperm count's as high as yours.'

Brian dismembered the wooden chair that came apart easily, and brandished a leg over his head.

'Go ahead.' Cindy turned up her square-jawed face for the blow. 'Open the curtains and let all those people out there in their cars see the spectacle of a battered wife.'

CHAPTER FOUR

❧

C.P. Games did not communicate again for long time, but another tiny postcard did turn up from H. V. Black Monk Trotman.

'Oo knows indeed?' he wrote. 'DeAth might look U up.'

❧

'Jack!' Brian called up the stairs. 'Look out of the back window.'

Jack was in his room, changing out of his walking kit. He was sitting on the bed in a velvet housecoat, wondering whether it was worth bothering with the bra and suspender belt for what was left of Sunday evening.

'Quick. There's a strange man going up the stairs to the flat.'

'A *man*?' As Jack, he would have been more interested in a woman, but in his complex Cindy guise, he was supposed to be mad for men.

By standing at the side of his bedroom window, he could see the underside of Tim's outside staircase without being seen. Feet were treading up, large feet in swollen trainers that looked as if they had been blown up with a bicycle pump. Above them, wide brown corduroys and a pneumatic green jacket.

At the top, the platform cut the man off from Jack's view. Downstairs, Brian heard the bell, and saw Tim's door open, and the man step slowly inside.

Cindy came down in the long burgundy housecoat, her feet in feathered mules.

'Tim's boy friend,' they told each other. It was no fun at all to guess that it was family, or a friend, or a man trying to sell insurance. 'We saw Tim's boy friend.'

H. V. Trotman's name was Harold.

'A fine royal name,' Tim said, in the mood of the medieval adventure games which were their common bond.

Surprisingly, Harold Trotman, such a craftily involved player in *Domain of the Undead*, did not want to talk about the games. He sat down at Tim's table, with his broad arms resting on the top and his hands turned down like paws, and waited for Tim to bring him a Coca-Cola. He looked like a beer drinker, but he wouldn't have a beer. Tim brought two cans, went back for mats, because he was fussy about his table top, went back for two packets of prawn-flavoured crisps, went back for salt and vinegar crisps because Harold didn't like prawn, went back for a saucer, which was all he had for an ashtray.

Harold smoked as if it were a career, taking long, careful drags, tapping the ash off with his forefinger, moving the cigarette about round the side of the saucer for best effect, picking it up purposefully for another intensive draw.

He did not look at Tim, so Tim was able to look at him. He had hair cut quite short over a large football of a head, growing low over his ears and forehead and quite far down the back of his neck, like fur. His face was blunt and stubbled. He had a long, weighty torso and short, thick limbs.

'I hope you didn't mind me writing to you,' Tim said. 'I wasn't trying to say you were cheating.'

Oh, that's all right.

Harold didn't say that, so Tim had to consider it said, in the pause.

'It was just that your metamorphosis into the Monk – it was very, don't get me wrong, brilliant, in fact.'

Thank you.

'But it was a bit of a dirty trick, you must admit, because it took away a lot of my points that I'd worked to build up over a long time.'

'That right?' Harold said, as if Tim had not already discussed this in his letters, and at some length with Kevin, Games Master at C.P., who made the rulings.

'Yes. I wish I knew where your next moves were going. But – er, but of course, if you told me, I'd counter them.'

Harold shrugged. 'Don't keep on about all that stuff.'

He occupied himself with lighting another cigarette. Tim took a pull at his drink. But if they were not going to talk about the games, what could they talk about?

They sat in silence for a while. The only good thing about Harold smoking so much (his clothes and body reeked like a public bar) was that he did not keep reaching into the crisps, so Tim ate them all. Harold had come knocking on his door just as Tim's jaws were open wide to close on a giant sandwich of liver sausage and pickles and cheese, and he had to shove it into the refrigerator and wipe his slavering mouth with a tea towel.

'My name is Harold Vincent Trotman,' H. V. suddenly began, and launched into his life story in a steady monotone, as if he were giving evidence.

That solved the conversation problem, but it was quite boring. Tim sat back with his feet on the bar of the table and listened and nodded and went, 'Ah-ha' and 'Mh-hm' when Harold said things like, 'Sixty, seventy bricks at a time, you won't find a man to carry more, and where does it get me?'

He fixed his gaze on Tim. There was some red in the white of the eyes, and a bit of a bulge.

'Superhod, the brickies call me. But will they put their money where their mouth is?'

'Er – no?'

'It's all part of the system, see. The way they got this country set up, you don't get a chance.'

The tale was ended. Should Tim tell his life story now? He opened his mouth, but Harold said, 'Well, that's that,' and got up, slapping himself for cigarettes. 'Got any?'

'I don't smoke.'

'Shan't be a sec, then.' Harold put on his puffy jacket again and went off, tripping and swearing on the loose step of the staircase.

He never came back. Tim waited ten minutes, and then dived for the sandwich and jammed it into his mouth, pickle juice running down his chin.

The next time Harold the hod carrier came, Tim was at work. Harold left one of his small cards under the door: 'See U Sunday, then,' as if it had been arranged.

Tim was supposed to be going to his parents', but he made an excuse, because he did not want to miss Harold. A strange, rather disturbing man, but they had *Domain of the Undead* in common, even if Harold would not discuss it. Was it a friendship? Tim had only one or two people he might call friends. He hardly ever saw them.

Harold did not come until four o'clock, so Tim could have gone for lunch at 23 The Avenue, Rawley. Fed up, he was sitting on the window-sill where he sometimes played at being a sniper at night, when he saw a white car pull into the gateway and stop in front of Brian's garage. Harold eased his broad frame out of it with some difficulty, like taking off a tight shoe, and lumbered towards the outside staircase. Tim waited until he rang the bell, and then counted seven seconds before he opened the door, so as not to look as if he had been spying down on him.

Harold had brought his own brand of soda, a six-pack of something called Cheerio. He offered Tim a taste, but it was spiced and syrupy, like fizzy cough mixture. Tim put out the doughnuts he had bought with the Sunday paper, and made tea, but Harold would drink only his sickly soda.

He was quite friendly, but rather suspicious. He wanted to know where Tim worked, why he lived up here ('like a chicken coop'), who lived downstairs, why Tim had written to him in the first place.

'Why me? Why pick on me?'

'I told you. I wanted to know more about the Black Monk. Players often write to each other.'

'Not to me they don't, they better not.'

'Why did you answer, then?'

'Ah.' Harold dropped his cigarette through the triangular hole in the top of his Cheerio can; it died in the dregs with a small sigh. 'I had to find out who you were.'

'Ah,' Tim echoed. He wanted to ask, 'And who was I?', but it might come out like a joke, and Harold was looking up at him seriously from a ducked head, while he lit his next cigarette.

'You can't be too careful, see,' Harold told him.

'I know.' Tim felt this himself.

'They after you too?'

'Who?'

'Anybody.' Harold looked over his shoulder at the window that faced the road.

Tim got up and pulled down the blind. 'You on the – I mean, don't get me wrong, and it doesn't matter if you are –'

'What?'

'On the –' Tim paused, and then said gently, like a question, to defuse it, 'the run?'

Harold leaned his weight back and laughed. The chair creaked and stood back dangerously on its inadequate hind legs.

'They haven't got me yet, son.' Harold banged the front legs down again and pounded the table with both fists. Good thing Brian and Jack were still out. 'No. You've got to be one step ahead.'

'That's right.' They were having a conversation, even though Tim was not sure what it was about.

'If they mess me about' – Harold took a great drag on his cigarette and swallowed the smoke, apparently for good, because it didn't come out – 'they know what to expect.'

'What will that be?' Tim asked politely, eating all round the edges of a doughnut to delay the glorious moment when the jam burst into his mouth.

41

'Well, there's a lot of things I'd like to do,' Harold said, not menacing, but in quite a chatty way. 'The royal family, for one thing. I'd take them out, for a start.'

'Why?' Tim was quite keen on the royal family, but he did not like to say so.

'Cost too much.' The smoke finally came out through the snouty nostrils of Harold's short wide nose that had not only a fuzz of hair inside, but two longer hairs sprouting from the middle of it, the same colour as the tufts of gingery hair on his cheeks. 'Could be done at the Tower. Quite historical.' He drew a finger across the sinews of his throat.

Tim cleared his own throat, but no words came out.

'Set a fire in the Lords, that would be quite nice. Westminster Hall, all those old beams. It would go up like a crematorium. Beautiful. You got to express your feelings, see. You get cancer else.' He put a whole doughnut into his mouth and chewed on it, musing. The red jam oozed out of the sides of his mouth like blood.

'Do you –' Tim cleared his throat again. 'Do you often think about that sort of stuff?'

'Yes. Don't you?'

'Well, I . . .' If this was to be a friendship, Tim could not say no, and sound like a wimp.

'That's right, of course you do. You don't think about my wife, though, because you don't know her.' He wagged a thick finger, explaining. 'My ex, that is, a real beauty, she is. And her family. If I had a gun, I'd blast the whole lot. You'd be the same.'

Struggling to keep up his end of the conversation, Tim was tempted to tell him about the imaginary night sniper who crouched on the window-sill. 'I sometimes I think – I think –'

'That's right, so do I.' Harold saved Tim from the mistake. He brooded for a while, with his arms weightily on the table. His reddish eyebrows lowered. He might be asleep.

Tim looked at his watch. He did not want Brian and Jack to come home and find Harold's car blocking the door of the garage.

Harold's eyes were open. 'Want me to go, or suthink?' he asked.

'No, I – no, of course not. I was just wondering . . .'

'Wondering what, old son?'

'Nothing. It's all right.'

'Wondering what?' One of Harold's bloodshot eyes was closed against the smoke from the cigarette clenched in his mouth. The other was fixed on Tim. There was a yellow ropey bit in the inside corner.

'I was just wondering if – well, since you like to think about – you know, those – er, things – is that why you chose to be the Black Monk? I mean, hack and slay, and that?' Harold's eye was a bulging stare. 'I mean.' Tim had seen role-playing games denounced in the papers. 'Does playing the games and that, does it make you feel, you know, vio – aggress – violent?'

Harold grinned. 'You missed the whole point. Keeps me out of trouble. Sublimates the urges, see. Keeps me from going out and chopping up babies.'

There was a banging on the door. Tim jumped up. 'Who is it?'

'Brian. Could you –' Mumble mumble.

Tim went to the door. Brian looked over Tim's shoulder to get a sight of Harold.

'Could you ask your friend to move his car? Sorry and all that.'

'No, it's – sorry, Brian.'

Tim looked back into the room. Harold was up and approaching, doing his bear walk. Brian clattered his boots down the steps. Tim shut the door.

'Got to go anyway, me old son. Thanks.'

'Thanks for coming.'

'All right, then?' Harold shrugged into his overblown jacket, which made him look like an American football player, and dropped a hand on Tim's shoulder. 'You're all right, considering.'

He tore open the door and pitched out. On the stairs, the broken step cracked and yielded. Harold let out a hoarse shout, 'Broke me bloody leg!', and crashed down. By his car, he turned round and waved. 'I'll sue!' he called up amiably. He went round the front of the car and fitted himself into it, backed out into the road and roared away. Tim shut his door before Brian drove in.

Considering what?

'Driving a car is erotic,' *Pocket Pickups* announced. 'You're controlling a powerful machine. You can be gentle with it, or forceful at speed. Get a car – get a girl!'

The powerful machine that Zara brought round before she left for Australia was a little old Fiat 650, known to her as Baby Bilious. The yellow paint had been patched in different shades, the bottom was fringed with rust, the aerial was a wire coat hanger, and bits of the interior had been eaten by dogs.

But it was a car. It was freedom, it was status, it was erotic. Tim loved it. He re-christened it Buttercup, and paraded about the local roads for a long, entranced time after he had driven his sister cautiously back to Rawley, and said goodbye.

Erotic, eh? He was a man with wheels, like everyone else. He was in charge. He conquered the miles. He could detest pedestrians, or make a benevolent gesture of stopping even before they had put a foot into the road, waving a lordly finger to let them cross.

Brian and Jack had said he could keep Buttercup in the space between the house and the garage, where there was just room by the foot of the outside staircase. Having fitted her in, he had to move his legs over the gear shift and get out of the passenger door. As he shut the door, which had a sticker on the window saying, EASY DOES IT, from Zara's days in Alcoholics Anonymous, and turned to slide underneath the stairs to get to them from the garden side, he saw Brian's girl friend with the rampant blonde hair watching him from inside the kitchen window. She was in the dark, but some light came through the doorway from the hall. She was wearing a pale suit with a pink scarf tied fussily at her neck; a rather nondescript type of woman, except for the hair.

Tim could not take the car to work, because there was nowhere to park unless you had a permit. After work, now that the March

44

evenings were lightening, he hurried home and changed into jeans and his bright-green sweater that would be noticed, and took the car out, as if it were a dog. Zara had had Buttercup for quite a while, and it had some irresponsible habits, which it must have picked up from her. The steering you couldn't take chances with. The wiper often stuck, and the gears were as erratic as Zara. Sometimes you could not get into reverse. Sometimes reverse was the only gear that worked smoothly. Zara had taught Tim how to fiddle the clutch, and he could always get into gear eventually, but there were embarrassing times when cars piled up behind him while he pushed and struggled to get into first, when a traffic light turned green. Not so erotic.

Sometimes he went on to the motorway and drove among the people sweeping along through the dusk to London, as if he were one of them, with an evening in town ahead. Buttercup could not reach any great speed, so he drove in the slow lane, making a serene face to show people that this was his choice. Any idiot could go fast, but there were philosophers and dreamers who did not need to compete in the self-destructive race.

When cars passed him going ninety or more, by his reckoning, he expected to find them stopped farther on by a police car with flashing lights, or piled up in a tangled wreck. Then he would be called as a witness to testify to the speed of the grey Mercedes under the arrogant hands of the white-shirted driver whose suit jacket hung on a little hook over the back door.

Once when he was tootling along doing no harm to anybody, a blue car which had been following him suddenly pulled out and passed him and then pulled in very sharply in front of him, as if expressing some sort of contempt. Tim had to brake. Anger rose in his throat like a hot undigested meal. Kill the brute! He was Harold, planning savagery he would never do.

The road rose up a slight hill and the man in the blue car had the nerve to slow down. Cars were passing steadily in the middle lane, but as soon as there was a gap, Tim gritted his teeth and pulled out to overtake the hateful blue car.

Buttercup didn't like hills either. With the accelerator on the floor, she strained, Tim strained, but the most he could do was stay level with the blue car, while behind him an enormous lorry snapped and snarled at his heels, and flashed its lights like dragon fire.

Getting back into the left lane behind the blue car, Tim struggled with fear and anger. He could not re-capture the poet-philosopher sense of relaxed superiority, so he turned off the motorway, to calm down on the back roads.

Buttercup ate petrol. Tim found that out, and had to cut down his conquests of long distances. He drove to local beauty spots and parked and read the paper, as if he were a salesman taking a break from a long day on the road. Once in a while, he would keep on his work suit, so that he could stop Buttercup among the group of cars browsing outside a pub and go in for a beer in his character as sales rep. If anyone spoke to him, he would indicate that he was on the road with the back of his car full of catalogues. He did not mind if no one spoke to him. What mattered was his own feeling of being this travelling man.

He took his mother shopping, because she could not drive now, nor get on and off the buses. Hanging on to the trolley, she could navigate the supermarket aisles, while Tim dodged ahead, getting things from the shelves and freezers for her.

On their way back to her house, Buttercup's gears jammed at a roundabout. Tim was sweating and desperate, but his mother sat there serenely, inventing reasons why the drivers behind them were getting hysterical (woman in labour, mercy dash with life-saving drug), and asking with curiosity, not malice, 'Why doesn't this happen with Sarah?', which drove Tim insane.

Growling in protest, the gears finally meshed, and they headed for home.

'Would it be too far to go round by the DIY, dear? I need a few things.'

Tim thought she would be buying scouring pads and light bulbs, but she bought things like emery-paper and glue and varnish.

'Why can't Dad get them himself?'

'He said he had to go off somewhere this afternoon. He's still pretty busy, you know.'

When Tim carried the shopping into 23 The Avenue, he found Wallace Kendall with his feet in narrow leather slippers on the table, watching a game of snooker on his wife's kitchen television.

What would it be like to have a father with whom you could joke in a pally sort of way, 'Busy, eh? And Mum and me running round to get all your rotten stuff.'

As it was, Tim unpacked and put away his mother's shopping, and carried his father's things out to the shed where he had his woodworking lathe.

'Be sure and lock up and bring me back the key.' Wally's shed was as sacred now as his superintendent's hut – kettle and electric fire steaming up the windows, flap table covered with overflowing ashtrays and carping reports – had been, on the building sites.

Jack was supposed to have mended the broken step on the staircase. He had not got round to it, so Brian came up to have a look.

Tim thought he was coming to ask for the second half of the rent, which was missing this month, because Buttercup had eaten into his salary with her demands for petrol and a new exhaust pipe when the old one got knocked off, backing into a high kerb. When he heard Brian at the foot of the steps, he wanted to pretend to be out, but the lights were on and the radio playing, so he had to open the door, his head seething with a stew of possible excuses.

'Need a whole piece of wood, that will.' Brian came into the flat. 'Your friend did it in, was it, the one in the white Escort with the pixie in the back window? He was a bit heavy for those stairs, if you ask me.'

'That step was broken before,' Tim reminded him.

'So it was. I did ask Jack, but you know what he is. I'm sorry, Tim,' Brian said, surprisingly for a landlord. 'It's not fair to neglect you, when you keep this place nice, and don't give any trouble.'

'That's all right, Brian. I'll tell my, er, my friend to be careful, next time he comes.'

'Comes a lot, does he?' Brian sat down on the bed that disguised itself as a couch with three cushions against the wall, and looked up at Tim thoughtfully, caressing his soft beard as if it were a lapdog carried high up.

'Well, I don't know, really. He's a – sort of – new friend.' Was it worse to know when a blush was crawling up the side of your neck, or would it be worse to have other people see you blushing when you didn't know it?

'I'm glad. Bit lonely here, is it?'

Tim shook his head dumbly.

'Bit hard to make ends meet?' Brian held up a hand. 'Don't worry about the rent. We trust you. Sit down.' He patted the bed. Panic rose. 'You're a good boy, Tim, a really nice boy, and I want you to know that if you ever need a friend – well, you've got your new friend and that's fine – but if you ever need someone handy –'

Tim had not sat down. A sledgehammer could not have made him. So Brian put both hands on his knees and stood up.

'Well, on my way.' He laid a shaggy woollen arm round Tim's shoulders and gave him a one-armed sideways hug.

Stiff as an iron bar, Tim stood still while Brian let himself out and ran down the steps, whistling. Tim remained rigid, his hands at his sides, staring at nothing. Help! he thought. I'd better borrow for the rent till I get my pay cheque. My *God*, he thought. I never knew.

So if Brian . . . Then was that why he and Jack . . . But Jack had that woman Janet Fox at work, who . . . Was he both? Were they both both? 'Good boy, Tim.' Did he really think that *Harold* . . .? And so he thought that Tim . . . But what about the girl friend with the yellow hair? Total confusion.

When he could move again, Tim tiptoed to the door and fastened the chain across.

Better get myself a girl friend. Out of the confusion, that thought emerged. Well, and why not? Having a car would make it easier. 'Your car can be transport, music centre, picnic venue, speed, excitement, privacy, bedroom. Get a car – get a girl!'

Frog-princess Lilian was married to a toad, but Gail was unattached, and had been reasonably friendly to Tim of late. They shared a few familiar jokes about Mr D. and Fred and the worst of the customers. That would be something to talk about, for a start.

Tim picked his time. Gail was quite passable, really, if you liked pointed noses with short upper lips pulled up towards them. She smelled clean too, and had a nice little way with customers, jollying the wobblies along towards the decision she had already made for them.

She had high pointed bosoms, like her nose. One day, she came to work in the same sort of pink jumper that Helen Brown had worn at the theatre, but it looked quite different.

'I was wondering.'

Tim took a deep breath and said it when they came out of Mr D.'s office together, after morning clothes brushing and collar straightening and Orders of the Day: 'Linens are going to be big this summer. When customers come in looking for cotton prints and nylon dress fabric, it's worth calling their attention to the pastel linens. Demonstrate the crush-proof qualities.' Mr D. made a crumpling movement with his hand, then fixed them with a no-nonsense eye. 'But be sure it's non-crush before you do that.'

'I was wondering, Gail – er, Gail.'

'Use her name often,' *Pocket Pickups* advised, 'as if you like the sound of it.'

'You were wondering, Tim – er, Tim?'

'Yes. I've got a car now, well, it's my sister's, really, but I've got it for six months.'

'That's nice,' Gail said brightly.

'Yes. And I was wondering if you – I mean, if you'd like to . . .'

She did not help him. She stood there outside Mr D.'s office with her head on one side and a slight smile hiding whatever she was thinking.

'I mean – I know you go out and I'm sure you've got loads of men, but perhaps you'd come – perhaps you'd have the time –'

'Ten past nine.' She looked through the glass door of the office at the clock on the wall, then back at Tim, with a grin.

'Don't, Gail. I'm saying, would you like to come for a drive sometime?'

She looked him quickly up and down. She was taller than Tim, and she made it clear that there wasn't far to look.

'Sorry,' she said shortly.

'Why not?' Don't blush, don't blush.

'You must be joking.'

He saw now that it was inevitable she should say that. It was one of those retorts available on a plate for a girl like Gail who could not even find an original remark to hurt you with.

Take off her head at the Tower, Harold. Tim pushed past Gail and walked ahead of her to an early customer at the rack of glazed chintz curtains with triple pleated headings.

'Can I help you, madam?'

So it would have to be Helen Brown. He had known that all along, and he had nothing against her, except that Val would take all the credit if he asked her out.

He did not know where Helen lived. He only knew that she worked at the Hall School. Something to do with the kitchen. He would go down there and look for her. What time would she come out? He could just see himself hanging about outside the chainlink fence and getting arrested as a child pornographer.

He thought about Helen, imagining her as better than she really was. He had to pretend that she was better than Gail. When he had worked her up into something quite passable, he took courage and asked Valerie where he could find her.

'I promised I'd lend your friend Helen Brown a book,' he said, when he went round to Val and Colin's place for a Sunday morning coffee. If you telephoned Val, she was always rushing off somewhere, or putting a meal on the table, and ringing off before you had said what you wanted.

'A book?' Her vampire's top teeth had been filed down and pulled back years ago, but she could still make them stick out over her chin when she wanted. 'You and she talked about books?' Val read books, you see, Val and Colin did. No one read books but them.

'She was interested in this particular book.'

'What book is that?'

'It's – well, it's about poetry.'

'*Poetry*? Helen Brown? She must have been putting you on. What else did she talk about? Did she talk about her son?'

'No. Should she have?'

'Oh no. No,' Val said airily.

In the end, Val gave Helen's address to Tim. She had no phone, but a neighbour took messages. Tim took the neighbour's number, but he could not manage this job as a third-party message.

One evening, he got into his car (it was not 'Zara's car' any more) and drove across the river to the tall, converted Victorian house where Helen lived in the top flat.

'It used to be the servants' rooms,' she told Tim, after she had come downstairs to let him in, and he had climbed the four flights behind her, trying not to notice that her thick calves ran down into her feet.

Helen had two bedrooms and a small living-room with shabby furniture and a big laundry basket of toys in the corner. The boy was away at school. The living-room had been painted by Val and Colin with three blue walls and one white one, which they had said was smart, and Helen agreed. The white wall was marked and smudged. It must be quite a small boy. How could he be at boarding school? Helen and Tim actually got themselves sitting down and talking a bit, but he could see that she was fussed about whether she ought to make tea. Her eyebrows were down. Two parallel vertical lines appeared over her nose and stayed there. Her pale lips were set.

'This is only a flying visit.' Tim stood up. 'I just wanted to know

– I've got a car now, you see, and I thought it would, I was wondering if you – I thought you might like to come for a drive out to the country at the weekend.'

'Oh, I would like to.' When she smiled, her eyebrows went back into place and the frown lines smoothed out. 'It's very nice of you, but I'm afraid I can't, really, because Julian is here at weekends.'

'Would he like to come too?' They could drive to Hamilton Park, walk around and look at the ducks and swans while the little chap was in the adventure playground.

'Well, no,' Helen said, 'not really.'

Amazing! She wants to be with me alone.

'Some evening, then? Why not tomorrow? It's light till seven.'

'All right.'

Helen came all the way downstairs to let him out, because the other tenants said that visitors could not be trusted to shut the front door securely.

'See you tomorrow, then.'

She did not smile. She just stood in the doorway with her legs slightly apart and her feet turned in, and looked at him seriously. While he went down the three cracked marble steps and along the path to the gate, she stayed in the doorway. He did not look back to see this, but he did not hear the heavy panelled door shut.

Pity his car was down the road. She would not see him swing into it. No, not a pity. For another twenty-four hours, she could imagine it as being something grander.

No offence, Buttercup.

The radio had long gone, leaving a rectangular hole down which Zara had stuffed her chocolate wrappings. Tim sang on the way home. As he turned in at the gateway, he remembered why it was so necessary to go out with Helen and for her to come to his flat, if she would. He had temporarily forgotten about Brian. The idea of the outing was important for itself.

He switched off the engine as soon as he felt the little bump of the front tyre that told him it had reached the concrete base of the stairs. Over the gear lever into the other seat and stealthily out of the passenger door, only half open so it would not scrape the house, and shut it silently. It hadn't locked since Zara had shut her keys inside and one of her friends had jimmied the door with a credit card. Slide under the stairs, leg round the end, and nimbly up to the top. Key in the lock quietly, ease door open.

Hallo there, Tim good boy. Wuff wuff. Where have you been?

Out to see my girl friend, so yah boo.

On the mat was a square envelope from C.P. Games. Tim bowed to it. He went in, shut the door gently, turned on the lights, took off his jacket and pulled the blinds, then went back to pick up the envelope and take out the papers for his next move in *Domain of the Undead*.

While he ate cold baked beans out of the tin, he checked his position and saw that Black Monk was up to no good at all, sublimating his urges like mad by poisoning Grue and slaughtering a harmless band of minor priests invented by a player called Cardinal Carcase.

'Using the basic codes,' the Games Master had written, 'show how Blch's followers will react when they meet the gurus and the sightless creatures. If they bargain, what with?'

'The weather-sayers have said,' Kev added, 'that flood tides threaten the Drear Lowlands. Forest fires are rife at this season. The mountain passes are still held by the forces of evil. Your next three strategies are crucial.'

Tim's head began to be full of ideas, but he did not start to fill out the forms right away, as he usually did, because he would not be able to work on them tomorrow evening. They would have to wait.

CHAPTER FIVE

❧

The whole thing was a total disaster. It was raining, for one thing, and another was that when Helen came downstairs to open the door, after taking her time, she looked like herself, instead of how Tim wanted her to look.

She wasn't even ready. 'Come up, I won't be long,' she said, but Tim muttered, 'I'll wait outside,' and sat in the car with his lip stuck out.

Helen came out under an umbrella. What had she been doing while he waited? She did not look any better. Her hair was still dry as a digestive biscuit, and she had done nothing to her face. No make-up. Tim had been brought up by Val and Zara to mistrust the naked face. She wore a dark-blue raincoat and broad stubby shoes. Tim would have stayed in the car while she got in, but he had to get out and open the difficult passenger door for her.

'"Easy does it,"' Helen said when he was back in the car beside her.

'You what?'

'The label.' She tapped the back of the AA sticker. 'I didn't know you were an alcoholic.' Of course, the drunken sailor husband. She would know about that.

'Good thing I'm not.' Tim was going to take her for a drink and a sandwich at a pub about twenty miles away that he had visited in his guise of sales rep, king of the road.

The Stag was crowded. They had to sit jammed at a corner table, with a man and a woman who belonged to a group at another table, and made a lot of noise and commotion about it. Helen did not want ham or beef, and when her cheese sandwich

54

came, she took the tomato out of it. Tim did not know her well enough to take it off her plate and put it in his beef sandwich, which had no tomato.

She drank a half pint of bitter so slowly that Tim had two pints, out of nervousness. They talked a bit, if only for the benefit of their noisy table mates. Helen spoke about the school kitchen, where the staff had a different job each week: chips and sausages, vegetables and fruit, pots and pans, dishwashing, serving hatch, out among the barbarities of the dining-room. After six weeks, you went back to frying chips.

Her voice was quiet. It was quite an effort to hear, but when you made the effort, you had to wonder if it was worth it. Tim told her a few things about Webster's, which she knew, because she had once worked there. Even while he was talking, trying to sound amusing, or at least interesting, Tim's mind and heart were yearning back twenty miles to his room under the roof where he would spread out his play-by-mail forms on the table and be himself, as Blch.

Helen finished her beer at last. Was it too soon to leave now? But he heard himself saying, 'Have the other half.'

('Buy her champagne. Find some excuse to celebrate and bring out the bubbly. It always works.')

'Should I?' The parallel lines were ravines in her forehead.

'Oh, definitely, darling,' said the older man at the table.

Damn you, keep out of this. But Helen shook her head. She had gathered up her bag into her lap, and looked as if she wanted to go too. Which of them was going to say it?

Two new arrivals were standing talking to the couple at their table, so Tim was able to say, 'Perhaps we should be moving along and let these people sit down.'

'No, no, don't think of it.'

'But really we –'

'Stay where you are.'

'Don't let us disturb you.' Helen stood up and went through the tables to the coathooks by the door. The rain had diminished

55

slightly, so Tim could drive a bit faster, although the wipers did not do a very good job. Helen put on her glasses, as though it would be safer if she could see too. Going up a hill, Buttercup flagged, so Tim did a flying change down into second to give her a boost. Or would have done a flying change if the gears had not stuck.

'Damn.' He pulled on the handbrake as the car began to move more backwards than forwards. Helen said nothing. Most women would be telling you what to do, or jittering because they thought someone was going to roar up the winding hill and hit them from behind.

At last Tim crunched dear little Buttercup into first gear. He was sweating, and his hand on the gear knob was trembling as he transferred it to the wheel.

'Sorry about that.' He glanced at Helen, as they started safely down the other side of the hill. She was looking ahead through her glasses. 'That's the only thing about Fiats. Always a bit tricky on the gears.'

'Are they really?' She believed it.

'Afraid so, but they're such brilliant little cars, and it only happens once in a blue moon.'

They were ten miles from home when it happened again. The lights were red at a narrow railway bridge, and they waited in a line of cars. The last car came over towards them. The lights changed. Tim followed the cars ahead up the rise of the bridge in first gear, changed into second – *back – into – second* – get in there damn you! – and with the terrible grinding shriek of an iron humanoid in agony, the gears jammed. Oh, totally jammed. Nothing like the minor difficulties of meshing that had once been so traumatic, but now seemed like trivia.

They were stuck on the top of the humpback bridge that was turned at right angles to the road on either side. The cars ahead had gone. The cars behind were eyes of light. Round the corner in front, a line of waiting headlights stared through slanting rain.

'What's happened?' Helen asked in a low voice, as if no one must hear.

56

'We've had it.' Tim got out into the rain. Mist and exhaust vapour rose white and red in the lights behind and before him. The traffic lights changed, and a car came up the narrow bridge from the other side, saw him and stopped. Behind it, someone sat on his horn.

Men got out and walked up the bridge.

'What's up?'

'The gearbox.'

'Stripped the gears, have you?'

'Bloody hell.' A man kicked Buttercup's back tyre. 'I'm in a hurry.'

'Can you help me push it?' Tim asked.

They laughed. 'Jammed in gear? Not unless you lift up the back wheels for us, mate.'

In the end, that was what they did. By this time, there were about ten cars on both sides. No time to wait for a tow truck. The cars in front backed out of the way. Helen got out of the Fiat and walked away under the umbrella. Four of the men lifted up the rear end of Buttercup, swearing and groaning, and trundled her like a wheelbarrow off the bridge. Someone had to steer and brake, so Tim had to sit in the car like a dummy while everyone else did all the work and said terrible things about him.

At the foot of the bridge, they pushed the yellow car off the road. Before Tim could thank them, they disappeared back to their cars and drove away. He got out. The traffic lights changed, with a small click from somewhere, from green to red and back to green. Cars waited, looking at him, then drove up and over the bridge. Cars came from the other side, and their headlights swept over him. He moved behind his car. Helen and her umbrella materialized out of the dark curtain of rain and stood beside him.

'Sorry about this.' He waited for her to start the sour grumbling and hissing complaints.

She only said, 'What do we do now?'

'Someone is calling for a tow truck.'

'How long?'

'I don't know.' He moved away from her, because he wanted to cry. Helen folded her umbrella and got into the car.

They rode in the cab of the truck that towed Buttercup backwards, her rear end in the air like a tart. From the garage, they rang for a taxi, and waited a long time. Tim did not apologize again. You can't go on and on saying, 'I'm sorry,' especially if the other person does not seem to mind. In the taxi, they sat at opposite ends of the back seat, leaning into the corners.

Tim had an uncomfortable thought. He cleared his throat and asked Helen, 'See Val much – my sister Val?'

'No. She did help me when I moved into the flat, that's all.'

Good. Tim did not want Valerie to know about this.

'Except just that one night, at the theatre. I suppose she only asked me to be someone for you. Or did she ask you to be someone for me?'

'Both, perhaps,' Tim said miserably.

'Yes, perhaps.'

By the time the taxi had dropped Helen and taken Tim home, the fare was enormous. Helen asked him in a quick whisper behind the driver's back whether he had enough money on him, and when he murmured, 'I don't know,' she took a ten pound note out of her bag and put it into his hand. His hand was sweaty and clammy, had been ever since Buttercup croaked on the bridge. Helen's fingers felt dry and bloodless, like gloves.

'Ley shaft bent. Two cogs completely jammed, and the teeth ripped. Whatever you did, you did a thorough job.'

'I wasn't driving,' Tim lied to the garage on the phone.

'I didn't say you were. Want us to go ahead and put in a new gearbox?'

'How – what will it cost?' Whatever it was, it had got to be done for Zara's car. It was Zara's car again now.

The new gearbox was going to cost about four hundred pounds, with labour. Who could he ask?

Not Brian, for a start. Tim had talked to him a few times since

58

the dreadful episode on the couch, and Brian had been his usual normal self; but a pass was a pass, and you didn't ask the passer to do you a favour.

Jack? Easy-going Jack with his jokes and his wide smile which he beamed on Tim if he ran into him on the offices floor at Webster's, taking invoices up for Mr D. Tim could not ask either of them, because he had only just paid the rest of the overdue rent, which he had borrowed from his mother, to keep Brian at bay.

So not his mother, for that reason. Also, she had been talking about getting herself a video recorder, but if you gave her the chance, she'd sacrifice that money on Zara's car instead.

The garage wanted a down-payment of two hundred pounds before they would start the work. Tim was desperate enough to go round to Valerie and throw himself on her mercy.

It was like throwing himself off a cliff. No mercy there. When Tim was a child, two years younger than Val, she was the witch of fairy-tales, the wicked stepsister, with her teeth and her nails and her stringy black hair and crowing voice. In a real story, the hero would have confounded her, stabbed her, beaten her into the ground, incinerated her into a puff of smoke. Tim made spells against her, but nothing happened.

Val got better after she grew up and went to college and got a job of some power and lived with Colin, but she could still revert.

Without telling her about the disaster of his night out with Helen, Tim asked her for a small loan, just a hundred or so, and really to help Zara, since it was her car and the gearbox would have packed it in anyway. Val stared at Tim over the ironing-board, drew her thin red mouth back into a snarling grimace and said, 'No.'

'Just – er, just no?'

'I have nothing to add.' She gazed at him through the thick glasses that protected her eyes and thoughts from your knowledge, like portholes protecting passengers from the sea. She thumped the iron about a bit, and then she suddenly put back her head and laughed.

'Don't look so glum, poor old Tim.'

'Were you joking?'

'I never joke about money. Nor does our Dad Wallace. You'd better go and ask him. You're his responsibility, not mine.'

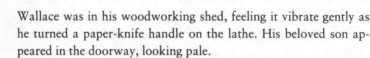

Wallace was in his woodworking shed, feeling it vibrate gently as he turned a paper-knife handle on the lathe. His beloved son appeared in the doorway, looking pale.

'Hullo, stranger,' Wallace said, as a way of letting Timothy know that his casual visits at long intervals had been noted.

'Sorry I didn't come last weekend, Dad. I had a lot on.'

'Who said anything about last weekend? We weren't here anyway. I took m'wife to the coast.' His son was the champion liar, but Wallace could lie too as necessary. 'Pass me that gouge would you? No, that's not a gouge. Up there, look, on the shelf. That's right, drop it. It only cost ten quid.'

'Talking of the cost of things, Dad . . .'

When the boy cleared his throat in that strangled way, it reminded you of those unwholesome programmes Annie loved – always on the BBC, since no one would pay to advertise on them – where the handicapped tried to walk and speak, and would have been better shut away and not embarrassing people.

'Is this a money talk, then?' Wallace asked, his mouth pursed, his skilled craftsman's fingers a marvel to see. 'Money talks.'

His son stayed mum, biting his lip. Wallace, merciful patriarch, put him out of his misery.

'Since you only ever come here to get a good hot meal or scrounge a bit of cash, I'm assuming, since it is neither lunch nor supper time, that you're after a loan.'

'That's right, Dad.' The worm squirmed.

'You know my motto. Never borrow, never loan.'

'I can pay it back. I get my bonus, end of next month.'

'Ah.' Wallace stopped the lathe and held the handle up to the light for Tim to admire. Tim was looking at the floor, and pushing shavings about with the side of his foot. 'So it's not just five pounds or so we're talking about.'

'Bit more.'

'How much more?'

Tim told him.

Wallace Kendall could not let his son continue with an explanation of what it was for. He could not trust himself, not with all these sharp tools about.

'You'd better go,' he said, with admirable calm, considering his whole blood supply was up in his head and battering to get out.

'All right, Dad.'

Why didn't the wimp stand up to him? Why didn't he say, 'Wait a minute, Dad,' and stand his ground, instead of ducking his head and fumbling his way out of the workshop? Boy couldn't even shut a door.

'Shut the bloody door!'

If Wallace Kendall had been Tim, he would have banged the door hard, and made the little hut shake. Tim closed the door as gently as if he were leaving a sick-room. His father started up the lathe again and the little hut began its gentle tremble under the hands of its master.

❧

In a wild flight of fancy, Tim imagined casting himself on the kindness of Mr D., and Mr D. would respond like a benevolent employer of olden times, remembering that he too had been young once and in need of a helping hand.

But the only helping hand Tim would get if he was insane enough to try to touch his boss would be a shove towards the door. Out. Sacked. Plenty more like you queuing up to get your job.

Zara, where are you? Zara would have rustled up the money from somewhere. Even when she was out of work and out of unemployment benefit, she always had enough for booze and drugs.

Harold, then. H. V. Trotman? Now there was someone who might have a bit of cash to spare in a good cause. He had a house and a car, and he must get decent pay as Superhod, whatever he said about the brickies. Tim rehearsed how he could possibly ask. Would Harold be angry with Tim? They were friends in a way. 'You're all right,' he had said, but would money destroy the friendship?

When Tim could not make a decision, he would sometimes consult the oracle. You opened the English dictionary at random, shut your eyes and stabbed a pencil at it.

Tim opened the dictionary somewhere under *h*, screwed up his eyes and let his pencil drop.

'Gimme a yes or no.'

The word was 'hamstring'. There you are – a direct sign from the oracle. Hamstringing would be in Harold's repertoire for the royal family and other ill-favoured persons.

He rang the garage. 'I'm O K on the deposit,' he told the man. The oracle cannot lie.

'You going to fetch it in?'

'I'll put it in the post. Will you order the gearbox?'

'When we get the cash,' the man said patiently.

Tim rang Harold several times before he got an answer. 'I've been trying to reach you for two days,' he said.

'Well, I've been here. Too wet to work.'

'Don't you answer the phone, then?'

'Sometimes I do, sometimes I don't.'

'I was wondering . . . well, I've not seen you for some time.'

Harold said nothing.

'I see you've been on the rampage. Black Monk, I mean.'

Heavy breathing showed that Harold was still there, at least.

'I gained a lot on the last grid, though. I was wondering – what about if I come round Sunday?'

'O K,' Harold said, gravelly as an old gangster movie.

Harold lived in an ancient market town gone high tech, at 'Marbella', Brentwood Close, a goodish walk from the bus station, on a new estate that ended in doomed green fields.

'Marbella', a semi on the circle at the end of the close, had an apricot front door guarded by gnomes, and window boxes and flowered curtains. Only the gnomes looked like Harold. He must have a woman there.

He did. As Tim went up the path, under the stares of two rude small boys in the garden on one side and a baby in a pram on the other, the apricot door opened, and an ochre-skinned woman came out in tight black jeans, with murderous sharp boots and hair fuzzed out like wood shavings.

'Hullo.' Tim smiled.

'Hullo.' She did not smile. Her mouth was painted on violet, in a heart shape.

'Harold in?' Tim knew he was. The white Escort was there, with the troll on a string in the back window, but he had to say something.

'Who are you?'

'His – I'm a – like, a friend.'

'Help yourself,' she said and went past him to the road, where she got into a red car parked behind Harold's. The tight black legwear made her bottom stick out, round and high.

Harold took him into a room full of heavy furniture upholstered in plaid velvet. Harold's ashtray, almost as big as a toilet bowl, was on a stand by his chair.

He did not offer any food or drink. 'Never let anyone put a foot into your home without putting something into their stomachs,' Tim's mother always said. Plumbers and electricians always got a legs-under-the-table tea, whatever the time of day. But Harold did not have that kind of mother. His was on his hit list.

While Tim struggled to find a path of small talk that could lead to money, Harold's veined protruding eyes roved round the room, looking too big for their sockets. When Tim finally dragged himself round to hinting at a loan, and then came right out with what it was for, Harold's eyes came to rest on his face.

He looked at Tim for a while and then he said, as if he were repeating a lesson, '*You* want *me* to loan you a couple of hundred quid?'

'That's right.' Tim nodded brightly. 'Just for a very short while. I get my bonus soon.'

'When?'

'You can't always tell, with Webster's.' Ha, ha, well we all know what *they* are. 'Look, I hate to ask you, Harold, but you're – well, I do think of you as a friend.'

'That so?' Harold dropped his cigarette end through the hole in the bowl of the ashtray. The stub must come out at the bottom of the stand. 'I thought I'd scared you off, previous.'

'Talking about – you mean, violence?'

'Yeah. You tell the truth to some people, they think you're psycho.'

'Oh, I don't.' Tim saw his chance. 'I mean – I don't blame you for feeling like that.'

'You'd back me up?' Harold looked at him over the huge hands that were lighting a cigarette. 'When the day comes that I finally let 'em have it – you'll be on my side?'

'Oh' – Tim crossed his fingers on both sides – 'definitely.'

Harold gave a grunt and suddenly disappeared from view, as the back of his wide chair went down and a footrest shot out.

'I'll pay you back, every penny, before you've even missed it,' Tim babbled to the yellowing soles of Harold's socks which were now up in the air. 'I'll work, I'll moonlight, I'll do evenings in a pub, mow lawns, clean cars. And look – not having Butter – my car for a few weeks – look what I'll save on petrol.'

Harold gave him two hundred pounds, in cash. He went upstairs to get it, and came down with the money in a neat, clean bundle, as if he had stolen it from a bank.

'Thanks – I mean thanks ever so.' The money burned in Tim's hands. Now that he had it, he almost wished he had not asked for it. 'You're a real friend. If there's anything I can do for you . . .'

'Pay it back.'

'Oh, I will, cross my – er, my heart.'

'Ten per cent interest.'

Tim had not thought of that. 'Of course.'

Could he take the money and run, or did he have to stay and talk for the look of things?

'Better get out before I throw you out,' Harold said, pleasantly enough.

Before Tim left, Harold produced one of his little cards and made him write out an IOU and sign it. Harold stuck the card in the frame of a picture painted on velvet of cows in blue moonlight in front of a ruined tower and a flat, reflecting lake.

CHAPTER SIX

When Tim sent off the money to the garage, he remembered that he should also be sending a ten pound note to Helen. He would get an envelope and a stamp from the office when Mr D. went to tea.

Mr D. did not take his tea break. One of his favourite customers, the wife of a famous racehorse trainer, was in the department, doing up a cottage for the stable lads, and Mr D., like a porpoise by the bows of an ocean liner, would not budge from her side.

Mrs Slade came in again. Tim liked her, and she liked him. Her husband hated the bathroom curtains, but she still came in from time to time to pick over the remnant tables or buy a bit of canvas seating. Tim gave her as much time as she wanted, while Gail thudded down another heavy roll of cloth on the table for a demanding customer, and glared at Tim.

By the time Tim and Mrs Slade had parted, mutually pleased, over a sample swatch of quilted lawn, and Tim had cleared up and checked his cash book, he was late knocking off. He missed his bus and had to wait for another, which was full. He did not think again about Helen's money until he was in bed with the light out, preparing the plot of a dream that he was going to try to explore.

Helen swam into his consciousness, standing meekly in her navy raincoat under the umbrella. Tim watched her walk away through the rain. He would not see her again, could not see her ever, after what had happened. She had been really nice about it, but she must be laughing her head off with the other women in the Hall School kitchen, as they fried mountains of chips and reduced spring cabbage to the consistency of wet laundry.

'Get a car – get a girl.' Helen had never been in any way a

possible girl friend. How ludicrous. But now there was no one again. No one at all.

'Don't give up,' *Pocket Pickups* said, in its reassuring 'I believe in you' way. 'You'll get snubs, sure, but you'll learn to say, "Your loss, darling," and go on looking for the woman who's looking for you.'

The next evening, Tim wrote to Willard Freeman again, just a chummy fan letter, just to stay in touch: 'Keep those books coming, Bill (that was how Willard had signed off, "All the best, Bill"). Your mate, Timothy (Varth) Kendall.'

The following evening, he wrote to Mary Gordon at the BBC. Anything was better than writing to Helen Brown and enclosing ten pounds.

'It was nice to hear you interviewing that woman who took her children across the Channel in a balloon.'

'Did you not feel at all nairvous about putting the wee ones through that risk?' Mary had asked, so sympathetically that the rather bold woman had broken down and admitted, 'Of course I did. I probably shouldn't have done it, really.'

Every day, Tim meant to send off Helen's money, and every day he didn't. Like walking back and forth past a crumpled paper on the floor and not being able to bend and pick it up, it had become one of those things he could not do. It wasn't the money. The ten pound note was already in the envelope and needed only a stamp.

An author had talked to Mary Gordon on the radio about having a writer's block. Tim had poster's block. The longer he left it, the harder it was.

Consulting the dictionary at *h* again, for Helen, he got the word 'healing'.

The money would heal her regret, anxiety, annoyance – whatever it was she felt about lending it. No. The healing would happen to their friendship, that's what it was. That was why he had not posted it yet, because the omens said that he was meant to take it to her himself.

I can't. You can. I can't. You must. She won't want to know.

Yes, she will, with ten quid in your hand. Tell her you couldn't trust it to the post, see? All these sorters' strikes. You've got to make sure she gets it. And then – honest, chivalrous you – you can thank her for being so nice about Buttercup.

But it was too far to get to Helen's place without a car. No, not too far, too boring. From Tim's side of town, it meant changing buses twice.

The school kitchen staff probably came out at the same time as the children, so that mothers working there could take theirs home. On the afternoon of his next day off, Tim went to the Hall School.

It was raining again. Was the combination of him and Helen a rainmaker? They should hire themselves out to Ethiopia. Come to think of it, it had been raining the night they went to the musical show. Helen had put a gruesome plastic bonnet over her head as they splashed from the pizza place across the ill-drained terracing of the new theatre.

Outside the school, women waited with toddlers sealed into pushchairs with plastic covers, like pork chops in the meat display. A school crossing lady held up her lollipop sign in the driving rain, and hustled large children across the road. No sign of any grown-ups coming out of the school. No sign of Helen Brown.

Tim hung about, head sunk into shoulders hunched against the rain, until most of the parents had walked away. A few children were still straggling out. The lollipop lady waited for them, shrouded to the ground in an enormous shiny white coat, with a sort of hood down the back of her neck and sticking out over the high peak of her hat. She looked totally ridiculous.

Tim went up to ask her when the kitchen staff came out. She turned, in the stiff heavy coat that seemed to stand up by itself, and a cold, pinched face looked up at him under the hood. It was Helen.

'Hullo,' she said, as if Tim were a father she saw every day.

'I didn't know you – what are you –'

The lollipop raingear had been made for somebody twice her size. Even the pole and the sign overpowered her.

'Excuse me.' She hoisted it up to stop a car, and shepherded two girls across the street. 'I do this as an extra,' she said when she came back, 'after we've finished in the kitchen. You're soaking wet.'

'I know. I've got your money.' The envelope was folded in his hand inside his pocket.

'Oh, thanks.' She looked surprised. 'That's nice of you.'

'Didn't you think I'd pay it back?'

She frowned and set her mouth. She looked so plain and pitiful inside the stiff white hood that Tim said, 'Do you – would you like to go out somewhere at the weekend? I won't have the car yet, but –'

'No, I can't. I'll have Julian with me.'

'Oh yes, I forgot.'

'But I'd like you to meet him. Look, don't give me the money now. The insides of these pockets are wet. Come up on Saturday and you can give it me then.'

When Helen opened the door to him, she was carrying, with difficulty, a boy of about seven, who was much too large to be carried.

Crippled legs?

'Should I take him for you?' Tim asked uncertainly, as Helen started to struggle up the stairs with the boy.

'No, I'm afraid he –' On the landing, she stopped to catch her breath. 'He's a bit funny with strangers.' At the top, she put the child down, and he ran into the flat on perfectly good legs.

'If I let him walk up and down the stairs,' Helen told Tim, 'he sometimes sits and screams and screams and won't move, and the people in the other flats don't like it.'

In the corner of the room, the boy had tipped all his toys out on to the floor and was sitting with the basket upside-down over his head.

'Come on, Julian.' Helen knelt and lifted off the basket, which he grabbed at fiercely and pulled down again. 'This is Tim,' she said to the basket.

69

The boy lifted the basket and hurled it against the wall. Tim noticed that the ornaments and pictures that had been there were gone. A blanket had been put over the television, and the mirror taken down.

The child had a beautiful face and romantic golden curls. With his head up, listening to something, he looked like a little prince.

'You're a nice chap, aren't you?' Tim felt very self-conscious, but he could not ignore the child in this small room, and Helen was watching him. He had to say something. 'How old are you?'

'He's autistic,' Helen said. 'I'm afraid he can't respond to you.'

'Aut – autistic?' Tim had not heard the word before. It sounded rather catchy, like something made up by people like Willard Freeman and Kevin Sills. The Auts could be a band of changelings. They were protected by their magical autistic armour.

'It's a form of brain damage,' Helen said, in the quick, clipped way she used for imparting information. 'In his case, caused by abnormal chromosomes.'

'I see,' said Tim, not seeing.

'He can hardly communicate, and he's very hard to control. That's why he has to be away at school. Didn't Valerie tell you? He was in her group when he was smaller, but they couldn't cope with him.'

Tim shook his head.

'I'm surprised.'

So was Tim. Val usually liked to spread any bad news. Helen frowned at him. Did she think that Val had not told this because it was so awful?

'I suppose she didn't think I'd see you again.'

'She didn't?'

Helen thought. Conversation with her tended to be in fits and starts. She said something, and you said something, and she thought about it. Then she said something, sometimes so short and quick that you could hardly catch it.

Julian was playing with a big coloured top on the floor. When it was spinning, he leaned far forward with his tongue out.

'Here – won't he hurt his tongue?' Tim saw the long, flexible tongue licking the top as it went round.

'He has to taste everything. I'll go and make some coffee, since he's occupied, if you'll watch him for a moment.'

Tim watched. Julian stopped the spinning top with a savage hand and chucked it against the table leg. When Tim went to pick it up and give it back to him, he saw that the legs of the table and the chairs were scarred and scratched. He also saw, from under the table, that the wire running from an outlet to the television was encased in a sort of rubber hose.

He crouched, and held out the top to Julian. The boy stared. Not at him. Not past him. Through him, as if Tim really were the invisible man. He watched, fascinated and horrified, as the child worked up a large amount of spit in his mouth, and then ejected it like a bullet on to the stained carpet.

He did it again. Tim got up and went into the kitchen.

'Can I have a cloth?'

'Oh, you are good.' Helen did not ask, 'What for?' She just gave him a damp cloth.

In the moment that Tim had been out of the room, Julian had taken off his clothes, all except a large nappy and plastic pants, which were tightly fixed on. He had a thin, agile body and long legs and lovely, healthy skin. He looked like a dream child.

He snatched the cloth from Tim and sucked it savagely.

'Here, give it to me.'

'It to me.' It was the first time Julian had spoken.

'No, to me.'

The naked child came towards Tim, legs apart in the ballooning plastic pants. Kneeling on the carpet, Tim held out his arms. Julian came close to him. Helen came in with the coffee mugs.

'Look, he likes me.' Tim felt triumphant.

Staring, the child stabbed out his fingers, and Tim jerked his head back only just in time to avoid having his eye poked out.

'He could probably see that light on the wall reflected in your eye,' Helen said. 'Things like that fascinate him. For a moment.'

71

Already the boy had backed away from Tim and was sucking hard on his own bare arm.

'How do you – er, sort of manage?'

'Search me.' Helen sat down with her coffee. 'I just do. I get some help, of course, in the holidays, but weekends I can manage. Spend most of the time cleaning up, and stopping him from wrecking the place.'

'Why do you have that wire covered? Does he suck that too?'

'He bites it.'

'*He bites it?*'

'He could chew right through it.' She laughed at Tim's shocked face, one of her brief, snorty laughs and blew out her pale lips, without a smile.

'Helen, I – I really, I mean, you're amazing, how you cope.'

'You get used to it. His father never did. That's why we split up, really. He couldn't stand me coping and him not.'

She spoke very fast, but Tim thought that was what she had said. No abusive drunken sailor then? It didn't sound like that.

'Will he get any better?'

Helen did not answer. 'Oh dear, Julian.' She made a face, and put down her mug. 'Come on, let's go and change you.'

'Change you.'

Washed and dressed again, he was still a lovely-looking child. He sat in a chair opposite Tim, jiggling his feet, winding up his hands, crooning to himself, a brief repetitive refrain, over and over.

'Julian,' Helen said lovingly. 'Julian.'

'Such a noble name.' Tim told her what he had thought. 'Such – such handsome looks. He ought to be a prince.'

'A sleeping prince,' Helen said. 'But no princess can wake him.'

Why couldn't I?

Julian rocked back and forth and appeared to ignore them both, but haltingly, Tim began to tell the child a story.

'Once upon a time, there was a golden-haired prince, who had a magic top. He could hang on to the top and spin himself away through space, anywhere he wanted to go . . .'

'He can't understand, I'm afraid. Autistics don't know about fantasy or make-believe.'

But I will teach him. I will lead him by the hand out of the dark enchanter's forest and into his own shining kingdom.

However, a trip with Helen and Julian to the supermarket was enough to make him decide not to have anything more to do with the sleeping prince.

'I hope you don't mind,' Helen said before he left, 'but I need a few things from the shops. Would you just come and help me with Julian?'

Getting Julian ready took about ten minutes. 'He loves to go out,' Helen said, but he became very agitated about his socks, and practically had a fit when she tried to put boots on him.

'No boots, no out,' Helen said firmly.

Tim held the strong struggling child while she forced short red rubber boots on to his feet (it was raining). She carried him down the stairs, and held his hand while they walked down to the main road. When Julian pulled back and tried to bend his knees and sink to the ground, Tim took the other hand and they pulled him along between them, his woollen hat over his eyes.

'Dragging the poor child along,' said a woman pushing a trolley towards the door of the supermarket. 'It's not good enough.'

'Can't she see –?' Tim asked.

'They don't want to know.' Helen had put Julian into a trolley, and it was Tim's job to keep him in it, while Helen scooted fast along the shelves to get what she wanted.

Julian threw out his hat. Tim picked it up. Julian threw it out. He pulled off one boot and threw it down the aisle. He let out a high hooting sound which made people look round, and then look away again.

When Helen came back, Tim went for the boot. Helen tried to put it on, but Julian screamed and raged and threw tins out of the trolley. In the queue at the check-out, people edged as far away as they could without losing their place. Nobody helped, or even

73

looked sympathetic. Tim wanted to tell them, 'He can't help it,' but Helen didn't, so evidently it wasn't the thing to do. While Tim was trying to stop Julian climbing out of the trolley, the child got an arm free and hit him hard across the face.

You bugger! If people had not been looking, Tim would have hit him back.

'Here – I'll take him out. You pay.' Helen gave Tim her purse and shopping-bag, picked up Julian and carried him out.

The rage that had made Tim almost hit the child merged into a giant blush. He put the shopping on the counter and paid for it and took the bag outside, the back of his neck on fire, feeling eyes on him.

CHAPTER SEVEN

❦

Willard Freeman did not answer any more of Tim's letters, so after a bit, Tim took him off his list of special heroes. Mary Gordon did not answer either, but that was understandable, for a radio star. She stayed on the list.

When Tim got his spring bonus from Webster's, he did not pay Harold back. He paid off the rest of the garage bill, and Buttercup came home to him, gears working like silk. Zara would be thrilled.

Life looked up. The sun came out and Tim drove his mother out for a picnic on the tow-path by the river. She did not want to get out of the car and sit on the grass, so they ate their sandwiches in the car park, and watched the swollen river sliding by, and people walking along the tow-path with dogs and fishing gear.

'That man is going to catch the biggest perch of the season. Look at his determined face. It will be stuffed and hung over the fireplace in his local pub.'

'Bad luck,' Tim said. 'He has to throw it back in the river.'

'He'll pretend he doesn't know that, and say it came from the reservoir. Look, that barge is full of old ladies from the Silver Threads. I can see them drinking tea.'

'This summer, I might get a boat.'

'And we'll cruise down to Henley regatta in style. Not like those two.' A man and a girl were labouring to row a small boat upstream. 'She's saying to him, "You call this a day out?" and he's saying, "You said the river was romantic."'

'I've seen just the boat I want. A little red cruiser in a yard near the wharf.'

But as usual, she was more interested in her invented dreams of strangers than in the reality of his.

Towards the end of April, the repertory theatre, the Boathouse, opened by the river wharf, and Tim was able to do a few jobs for them, as he had last year. Mostly it was selling programmes and showing people to their seats and locking the fire doors after the show.

This year, there was a cheerful, burly young man in the company called Craig Reynolds. It was his first year in repertory, but he performed small parts well, and was very friendly to everyone at the theatre. The ushers usually did not have any contact with the actors, but Tim sometimes stayed late on Saturday to help get out the old set and fit up the new one for next week, and Craig was one of the assistant stage managers.

'You here again?' Craig said to Tim as they were getting out the set of *Poor Lucy*. 'You give a lot of time to this place.' Tim signed himself up to usher as often as possible, partly because he did not want to be at home if Harold came round looking for his money. 'Great to see such enthusiasm.'

'I saw the play four times this week,' Tim said. 'I like that bit where you're cornered, but the audience still doesn't know you've done it. "That's right, you fools."' He lifted a light door off its hinges and put it down to declaim. '"Waste your time with me, while the real murderer is probably miles away by now. If you want a – a scape – a scapegoat, look into your hearts to see who really killed Lucy Grainger. You – all of you, with your smothering protection and your pills and therapists that turned a normal, bright girl into a zombie!"' It was so much easier to say someone else's lines than to talk out of your own head. '"I loved her, do you understand? I – (Craig's break in the voice) I loved her!"'

'Jolly good,' Craig said. 'You should have done the part instead of me.'

Tim put Craig on to his specials list.

Harold had rung him up a few times, and had come round once and made a bit of a scene. Tim had pretended he was shampooing the rug, and would not let him into the flat, so Harold made the scene on the small platform at the top of the stairs, and Brian had opened the kitchen door and called up, 'If you break that step again, you can mend it yourself!'

Tim had made up some promises that Harold seemed to believe, and when he had gone away grumbling, Brian came up and said something unsettling about rough trade.

Tim would have to invite Helen up here soon, for the look of it, but he was not sure whether he wanted to see her again. Without Julian, she was passable, he supposed, although she was about six years older than him, and looked it. He thought about Julian a lot, with fascination, but also with fear. It had been terrifying to realize how easily he could have hit him – hard.

Tim puzzled about the strange child.

'Can't do make-believe,' Helen had said. What must that be like? 'He probably can't imagine the past or the future,' she had told Tim.

He sat down and cleared his mind and tried to live in the present moment, to see what it would feel like. It couldn't be done. Images from yesterday, last year, this morning, words, people, thronged at the edges of the mind and spilled over into it. Thoughts raced ahead. Tomorrow's Thursday, stock-taking. Next week, *Private Lives* starts at the Boathouse. Only principals. Craig won't have a part. I wonder if he'll be doing front of the house. Must think of a joke for him in case I see him. Two days ago, I had that lovely steak and kidney pie. The gravy bubbled up through the crust. When I've finished this nonsense, I'm going to have some bread and cheese.

Five minutes without imagination? It was impossible. Helen must be wrong about Julian, just repeating some rubbish the doctors had told her. There must be dreams and memories behind that princely brow, and Tim could unlock them if he chose. But after the supermarket, he was not sure that he did choose.

He watched the dress rehearsal of *Private Lives* with the other ushers and staff families, and afterwards he found Craig on the grass bank by the river, throwing bread at the ducks and swans.

The ducks were vulgar opportunists, but Tim loved the swans.

'Royal birds.' He sat on the grass and admired Craig's agreeable looks in the sun. The swans carried their beauty above the surface, sailing magically. Below, the dark water hid the ungainly angled legs and splayed feet that propelled them. Tim stretched up his neck to try to imagine how it would be, and turned his head stiffly, blinking his eyes.

'I was a swan in a former life,' he told Craig.

'How do you know?'

'Oh I – just know.'

'*I* was only a lump of ooze. Are you psychic?'

'Oh yes.' Tim would say anything to get Craig's attention.

'I'll pay you in May,' he had promised Harold. 'Cross my heart.' He did pay off some of the debt, and decided to put the rest out of his head until he could save some more, or sell something. Sell the television? He couldn't see himself going downstairs to ask Brian and Jack if he could watch the late films. They went to bed at ten, because they got up early to have a jog round the park in orange track suits. Once, walking early after a nightmare, Tim had seen the girl friend going out at dawn with Brian in the same colour suit. Perhaps she had borrowed Jack's.

As May got warmer, there were more boats on the river and people strolling on the streets with open faces, instead of pinched and hurrying. Tourists came to the town to look at the cathedral and its close and water garden.

If visitors looked lost, frowning over maps, Tim might offer help, and even go a short way with them, enjoying the brief contact with strangers, liking to be seen as a knowledgeable native. At this time of year, he sometimes went into the hushed, aloof cathedral and knelt down, pretending to pray, as a bit of local colour for the tourists. Their voices became quiet, their steps softer, impressed with the *devoutness* of this place.

There were printed guides to the cathedral, but they cost two pounds, so most people just wandered round and looked at random.

If they were lucky, they met Tim, ready to invent for them the saga of Sir Leonard and Lady Margaret, inviting them to feel how the stone of the garments was worn away, like the toe of St Peter in Rome, by the hands of bygone generations who believed this would cure arthritis.

Or they could find him on the bench opposite the pitted wooden crucifix, moving down to the end so that they could sit down with him and contemplate the sorrowing figure of ancient days.

He might ask Americans if they had heard the legend.

'Why no.' They pricked up their ears like dogs for a biscuit.

'It's been said – it's only a legend, mind (in case they bought a guide or asked a verger) – that a sixteenth-century monk, after intense meditation here, was seen with blood on his hands and feet.'

'Gee.'

'Some people believe that's still possible.'

Tim's hands were clenched on his knees, so they could remember that afterwards, and wonder . . .

At the end of May, Harold was waiting in the brick-paved alley at the back of Webster's. Tim came out of the staff door with Gail. They were going to walk to the card shop and get a card for Fred's birthday.

Harold walked with them. Tim kept himself between Harold and Gail.

'All right, come on.' Harold clicked his fingers. 'Let's have it.'

'I told you, by the end of the month.'

'It is the end of the month.'

'I meant next month.'

'Sod that,' said Harold, and Gail poked her head forward across Tim and giggled. 'I'll beat you up. I'll murder you.'

'Are you –' Tim stopped and faced him. 'Are you threat-threatening me?'

'What do you think?' Harold's eyes were fiery boiled eggs. 'I'll cook your kidneys.'

'I could report you,' Tim said. 'Uttering mena-menaces – there's my bus!'

He broke away and ran across the street through the traffic and hopped on a bus going in the wrong direction.

Next day at work, Gail told him, 'Timothy Kendall, you're getting quite weird. What are you up to? Who was that man?'

'Nobody. He's always trying to borrow money off me.'

'He's got a hope. Ugly-looking customer, though. I nipped into the arcade till he'd gone. I got the card, no thanks to you.'

It was a huge birthday card with gold borders and a raised pink-satin heart. They all signed it, even Mr D., and put it in Fred's drawer.

He had a little weep when he found it, his lumpy blue lips trembling.

'Getting past it,' Lilian said, meaning Mr D. to hear.

Tim pushed her against a stand of heavy leatherette.

'Do you *mind*?' Being broad-based, she didn't topple. She righted herself by clutching at Tim's sleeve, pulling his jacket half off.

Tim was quite shaken by the ambush at the staff door. If Harold was going to stalk him, life would not be worth living.

'If I had a gun, I'd blast the whole lot,' he had said that time in the flat, when he had revealed his secret dreams and rages. Would the next thing be a chunk of concrete dropped on Buttercup's roof from a bridge over the road, or a bullet pinging through the gabled window of the flat?

When the papers for his next turn at *Domain of the Undead* arrived, Tim was even more uneasy. Blch and his daring raggle-taggle army, who had taken possession of the settlement at the very foot of the hill fortress, which might or might not hold the swift zoetic rapier, had been overwhelmed by a sudden influx of new and powerful characters attacking them brutally from the rear. Vrage, Vrevolta, Gorescalp – where had they come from? Some player had poured a lot of money into the game to buy the forms to create and control all these new ghastlies. Someone very vindictive and cunning. One of the new ravagers was called DeAth.

Tim wrote to Harold. 'This is a letter because my phone is out of order.' He had been leaving it off the hook a lot of the time when he was at home. 'I'm the victim of a dastardly plot. Are Vrage and Gorescalp all yours?'

In return, the small card's tiny writing, so unlikely from the large hod-carrying fist, told it all.

'Got it in 1. Blch & co is doomed. Y not give up?'

Tim sold his television set to Jack, who wanted an extra one for his bedroom.

'How will you get along without it, being on your own?' Jack asked.

Tim shrugged. 'Mostly it's rubbish.' Implying: some people lie in bed and watch that crap through their toes. 'I'm studying.'

'What for?'

'To better myself.'

'Good for you.' Jack was such a nice fellow. He had a wide, comfortable smile and good spirits in his eyes. 'So am I. Tough, isn't it? There's a management training programme in the Accounts Department at Webster's, you know. Do you want me to –'

'I've talked to them.'

'Who did you see?'

Panic. 'Mr – Mr Wood.'

'He left last year.'

'That's when I talked to him.'

Jack wrote a cheque. Tim cashed it and took the eighty-five pounds to 'Marbella', Brentwood Close, and gave it to the woman with the high bottom and violet lips.

He was furious with Harold. True, he owed the money, but he was angry about the threats and dirty tricks. Little Hitler had droned to him in the shed, over the drone of the lathe, 'Never borrow, never lend. Borrowers end up hating the lender.'

Dead right, Dad, as usual. Ever been wrong? But if a person could never be humble, he could never be humiliated.

Tim did not go to the Boathouse that week. They had an influx of interloping drama students, and did not need him.

One evening, as he sat on his low window-sill and picked off the unheeding cars – ping, ping, ping, with an air rifle disguised as a toilet plunger, the nine o'clock news came on the radio. Tim was not listening. He was in a dazed dream, hypnotized by keeping aim at the cars, but, as the news reader plunged dramatically into the lead story, he lowered the plunger.

'Reports are coming in of a sniper terrorizing the Green Ponds housing estate near Heathrow Airport. Two children and three adults are known to be dead, and several other people have been rushed to hospital with severe injuries.'

A sniper . . . and I was playing at guns through the window. Or was I playing? What are they talking about? Tim shook his head to try to clear it. What's happening? Are they talking about me?

'. . . and the man, in his twenties or thirties according to eye witnesses, and carrying a sub-machine-gun, appears to have escaped. Police are on the scene. Details are still confused. We'll keep you up to date as more information comes in.'

Tim sat thinking about it for a long time, with the plunger across his lap.

Next day, the senseless, horrible crime was on everybody's lips. Four people had been cut down in the street, and one more had died in hospital. Three were wounded. One was in a critical condition. The man, a local resident, who had tried to escape in a red car, had crashed into a police roadblock and was dead. His name was Barry McCarthy. He was unemployed, a loner. No one knew anything about him. As they would say about Tim.

'Makes your flesh creep.' Gail and Lilian were excited and jumpy. They jabbered together, instead of getting dustsheets pulled off and folded.

'I might have been there,' Gail said. 'That's not far from where my cousin lives. Suppose I'd been there? Look at his picture, those staring eyes.' They were ordinary eyes, and the picture, taken some years ago, was blurred.

'He does look a bit familiar, though,' Tim said, in the casual voice he used for inventing. 'I could swear I've seen him. Here, perhaps, in the store.'

Gail squealed, and Lilian said, 'Knock it off, Tim.'

Tim prowled the aisles between the tables and the racks of cloth rolls and hanging samples, brooding on the terrible event. Two children walking home with their mother – all shot outright. A man with his dog (the dog had survived: they had its picture). What sort of maniac would do a thing like this?

A sort of maniac like – wait a minute, suppose Harold had . . . No, of course not. They knew the man, Barry McCarthy, and he was dead.

But if it had been Harold, Tim would have been a star witness.

Tim decided to go down to the Boathouse anyway, and he had a beer and a bit of a chat about the crime with the barman during the first act. He felt out of it, not having a job to do, being only a customer.

Sheila, the front-of-house manager, came through the foyer. 'Didn't expect to see you, Tim.'

'Just thought I'd come down to see if you needed a hand.'

'Can't stay away, can you?'

In the interval, he hung about on the boarded terrace between the theatre and the river where the audience walked about with drinks and discussed the play. Tonight he heard many of them talking about Barry McCarthy. One of the wounded had been discharged from hospital. One was worse. Tim sneaked into an empty seat in the gallery for the second act, and stayed on to count the ice-cream and coffee money for Sheila. He went through into the theatre to look for lost property. Craig was at the side of the stage, checking a music tape that had not cued in at the right point.

While Tim went forward along the rows, they talked back and forth, about the play, and about Barry McCarthy and the Uzi gun. Everyone was talking about Barry McCarthy and Green Ponds.

'Good thing he's dead,' Tim said.

'Not really,' Craig said from the stage. 'The psychologists could have had a field day, trying to find out what makes a quiet man suddenly do a random, violent thing like that. Now they'll never know. Nobody seems to know anything about him.'

'I do,' Tim said suddenly.

'*You?*' Craig looked down at him as if it were a joke.

'Well, yes, I do, as a matter of fact. But it's nothing. Not important. I'll keep it to myself.'

'No you don't.' Craig jumped down from the low stage and pulled Tim upright as he was bending under the third row to pick up a lipstick.

'Well . . . one of the things I do (as if he had innumerable pursuits) is a sort of, you know, sort of role-playing adventure that you play by mail. Carrier Pigeon Games, they call it.'

'Sounds fascinating.' Craig pushed down a seat and sat on it. 'Go on.'

Tim leaned against the back of another seat. 'It sounds daft, but this man, Barry McCarthy, he was involved in it too.'

'You met him?'

'No, but I knew he was in it. Point is, everyone's saying he was such a quiet man – never harmed anyone. But he invented this really wicked character, see?'

Craig was absorbed. He leaned forward, hands on knees, nodding rapidly.

'Black Monk. An evil friar. Killing was his bag. Cut down, hack and slay.'

'Barry McCarthy?'

'Yeah.' But it was Harold's face Tim saw above the monk's black blood-stained robe, moving mercilessly through the forest.

'My God.'

Having made his effect, Tim went along down the row. 'It's only fantasy, after all. Not important.'

'Oh, but it *is*. This ought to be reported.'

'No, don't tell anyone. This is just chat. I thought it would amuse you.'

'I am not amused.' Craig stood up. 'I'm horrified.' He looked at Tim attentively. Then he nodded and said, 'Thanks,' and went away up the aisle to the front of the theatre.

'Good God, who's that?'

Jack and Brian were up, Brian making the tea, and Jack at the table with a dressing-gown over his night-dress, reading the paper.

Two pairs of feet were going up the stairs to Tim's flat. It was not yet eight o'clock in the morning.

'First, our boy has no visitors at all. Then he has this stream of men with big feet up and down the stairs at peculiar hours.'

'Police.' Brian lifted the tea-bags out of the mugs and flipped them into the bin. 'They're on to you at last, Cindy dear. You'd better run up and put your trousers on.'

Actually, it was the police. Detective Sergeant Miles, Special Squad, and Detective Constable Something, incident room, looking for Timothy Wallace Kendall.

Tim was both terrified and thrilled. The two men produced their warrant cards, just like in a film. One part of Tim wanted to hold out his wrists for the handcuffs. Another part wanted to crawl back into the bed that had not yet been made into a couch. Another part ducked his head and said, 'I've got to get ready. I'll be late for work.'

'Shan't keep you long, Mr Kendall.' The Detective Sergeant had hair like corrugated iron. 'Just like to ask you a few questions.'

'Would you –' Tim indicated the table and chairs. His coffee was cooling on the counter and the thermostat on his toaster didn't work. He wanted to get nearer to it.

'That's all right, Mr Kendall. Shan't keep you a moment.'

They knew about *Domain of the Undead*, and about Barry McCarthy and Black Monk. Craig had taken Tim so seriously that he had gone to the police.

It was tremendously dramatic. The police had come to Tim to

hear something they did not know about an important crime. Well, of course they didn't know it, because it wasn't true. The Detective Constable produced a witness statement form and sat down on the window-sill to fill in Tim's name, address, date and place of birth.

'Occupation?'

The toast began to burn, and Tim got away to the other end of the room, had a quick gulp of coffee with his back to the policemen, and got his wits together.

'We'd like to take a statement from you, Mr Kendall.'

Tim took a deep breath. Something about the imperturbable eyes of the two men made it impossible to say anything but, 'I, er, I'm sorry, but I'd better tell you. What you were told I'd said, well it isn't really true.'

'You didn't say it to Mr, er, Mr Cwaig Weynolds?'

You didn't often meet a policeman who couldn't pronounce his *r*'s.

'Yes, I said it, but it – well it wasn't strictly true.'

'Is that your statement?'

'Yes.'

'Would you like to vewify it?'

The words on the form blurred in front of Tim's eyes. He nodded miserably. He had let it go. He had lost it, the drama of being a witness.

'Thank you. You know, Mr Kendall,' Detective Sergeant Miles said pleasantly, 'wasting the time of the police with false information is an offence.'

'Oh – I – oh, but I –' Tim felt his mouth opening and shutting like a fish.

'It could bring you before a court.'

'But I didn't give you the information,' Tim said desperately.

'That's true, but given the nature of the crime involved, it could be assumed that you knew that Mr Reynolds would not keep your information to himself.'

'I'm sorry.' There was nothing else to say.

'Don't worry.' The Detective Constable stood up. 'There's thousands like you,' he said stoically.

'You mean, people who –' The drama had vanished. Tim was only one of humdrum thousands.

'Oh, yes, do it all the time. Most of them confess to the cwime itself.'

'They do *that*?'

'All the time.' The man sighed and looked at his watch.

'Why?'

'Why did you tell Mr Weynolds about the fantasy game?'

'To amaze him,' Tim said plainly. He had been jolted out of nonsense, but even so, he liked hearing himself give the simple honest answer.

'Well, then.'

The two policemen left. Tim's mind raced ahead of them to the station. He would walk in with his small head high – when he was in his teens, he used to measure it constantly to see if it had grown – courageous.

I'm the man you're looking for . . .

'Everything all right?'

As Tim stood at his open door to watch the detectives' car drive away, Brian called up from the garage. 'You've got early-bird friends.'

'Yes. Haven't I?'

'Thought you'd got the bailiffs in.' Brian pushed up the overhead door and went inside.

I'm the man. At the desks behind the high counter, heads would lift, pens in mouths, a stir.

Come off it, Tim. They've got him, remember? He's dead.

Brian's car backed out of the garage. Jack came smartly out of the back door, pulled down the overhead door and got into the car.

Tim brushed his hair, put on his tie and jacket, left the flat untidy, with his cold coffee and burnt toast, and was ten minutes late into the department.

'Late on parade.' Mr D. fussed. 'It throws the whole operation out of gear. I may have to ask you to stay an extra ten minutes this evening. Your excuse, please.'

Just this: I was helping the police with their inquiries.

But he would never tell. Torture me, Mr D. Put upholstery tacks under my nails. In the incident room, our lips are sealed.

CHAPTER EIGHT

❧

A green Webster's envelope came through Brian's letter-box. Tim's rent money. He usually knocked, and handed it over.

Brian opened the door. 'Why so furtive?' Tim looked as if he had been caught ringing bells.

'I thought you were both out.'

'School holiday.'

'Oh yes, of course. Well . . . it's all there.'

Poor little devil, he had been late with it only a few times in his tenancy. 'I'm not worried,' Brian said. As Tim turned to go, with that nervous duck of the head, he asked him, 'Everything all right?'

'What? Oh yes, thanks.'

'It *was* the police, though, wasn't it, the other morning?'

Tim shook his head. But the lie was a lost cause.

'Come on, I can tell the flowerpot men by their feet.'

'Parking offence.' Tim was at the end of the path.

'Remember,' Brian gave him the trustworthy smile, 'if you ever need help . . .'

He stood at the door and watched Tim walk away fast to the bus stop, thin, young, not quite filling the dark suit, the back of his neck, where the hair's edge was clipped too high, vulnerable as a baby.

Not fair to play games with him. It should have been funny, but it wasn't.

❧

Pocket Pickups, page 92: 'Don't ignore the plain, unattractive girl. Chances are, she will be warmer and friendlier than the girl who can have any man she wants. She needs to be. Look inside, not outside, and if you really can't stand the outside, treat her to a professional make-up and hair-do, and a really sexy outfit.'

Oh, Helen, by the way. Tim could just hear himself. I've made an appointment for you at Beautyworks. After, we'll go to Ladies' Fashions at Webster's . . .

'Oh, Helen.' He had left a message with the neighbour, and Helen had rung him back. 'I was wondering. Haven't seen you for a while.'

'And the last time was so awful. With Julian. I thought you'd never want to see us again.'

'Oh, well. Well, I'd like to.' She must be waiting for him to say, 'I want to see *you*,' but in an odd, compulsive way, he did want to see the child again. The sleeping prince. The boy who would never get into trouble for making up stories, since stories were not a part of his detached world. 'What about Sunday? I thought perhaps you might like to come to my place.'

'Oh, Tim, that's nice of you,' Helen said in a rush. 'But he can't go on buses. He gets fetched to and from the school.'

'I'll fetch you, then.'

'No, I'd worry about your flat.'

'Well, he couldn't bite through the cable of the television, because I haven't got one.'

'He'll mess the place up.'

'I wouldn't mind.' Brian and Jack might. It might undo the benefit of seeing a woman's legs – even Helen's thick ones – going up the stairs.

'You've got no idea. You come here. What about Sunday afternoon?'

'All right. I'll bring the supper.'

'Thank you.' Helen rang off, and Tim went into a state of anxiety that would last until he had actually bought the food on Saturday.

*

No, he had no idea. His memories of Julian had been softened into a few bits of odd behaviour and a temper tantrum in the supermarket.

The child had a slight cold, so as well as spitting, he blew his nose, not even into his fingers, but snorting straight on to the carpet or the furniture or your knee, whatever happened to be in the line of fire. He dragged off his shorts and nappies and smeared their contents on the wall.

He came back from the bathroom with a soapy sponge. He soaped his arms and hair and tongue and the legs of furniture, and Tim's hand and arm, when he went to sit by Julian with his sleeve rolled up. Then he threw away the sponge and made patterns in the sticky soap on Tim's arm.

Being touched by this electric boy was pleasing, flattering. Tim wanted to hug him hard, and force understanding into him with the fuel of love. He did manage to hold the restless body briefly, before Julian scrambled back and hit him in the stomach with a soapy fist.

'You've got to think ahead of what he's going to do,' Helen said, coming back into the room. 'Like a boxer. Did he hurt you?'

'No,' Tim lied.

'You're quite good with him. Most people are either scared or embarrassed.'

'I like him.'

'Honestly? I mean, I love him, of course, but that's different.'

Tim had brought Julian a little toy car. When he gave it to him, the boy opened his fingers and dropped it and walked away, which Helen said he always did with presents.

They put Julian in a corner of the small kitchen with the car, and he pushed it, not in imitation of a car, but to and fro obsessively, while they got the supper ready.

'Turn up at her place with champagne and smoked salmon and a few long-stemmed roses.'

Tim had brought a bottle of Bulgarian wine, veal and ham pie slices, lettuce, potato salad and French bread from the delicatessen counter in Webster's restaurant, and a packet of fish fingers, because Helen had said Julian liked them.

'You're very thoughtful.' Helen looked round from the frying pan and smiled.

Don't blush, Tim. It's only Helen. He was opening the wine. Thank God it had a screw top. He poured a glass for each of them.

'This is quite nice,' Helen said. 'I feel comfortable with you.' She sometimes said things like that, very direct.

Tim was working himself up to saying, 'I do with you,' when Helen put down the glass and the frying spatula, and dived across the room to rescue the small car which Julian was about to hurl through the kitchen window.

At the table, Julian, in a vinyl bib as large as a surgeon's apron, picked all the breadcrumbs off the fish fingers to see what was underneath. He ate some of the fish with his fingers, and wiped them on his hair. He grabbed for a radish, stopped chewing when he found it was hot, and exploded it over the table.

Tim and Helen ate fast, that was the trick, to get in enough between attending to Julian, and to stop him taking food off their plates. They kept their wine glasses on the bookshelf behind the table where he couldn't reach them.

Helen put on some music, and Julian slid off his chair and danced in a strange, jerky way, while Helen and Tim drank their wine and gave him applause. Did it mean anything to him? That did not matter. Giving it was the point.

'His hair's much too long,' Helen said.

'It's beautiful.' The softly curling golden hair hung over the child's face, as he sat by the cupboard door, opening and shutting it in a dedicated way.

'It wants cutting, but no barber will take him. Do you think you could hold him still while I have a quick chop with the scissors?'

They sat Julian in a low chair and Tim knelt in front of him, with the boy's legs between his, and his arms round the taut, suspicious body.

'Once upon a time.' He would never give up the quest for the grail of Julian's soul. 'Once upon a time, there was a prince who didn't like to have his hair cut.'

'Hair cut.' Julian did not connect it with himself.

'It grew so long that it was down his back and all down the front of him like a tent, and birds used to nest in it and sing as he moved about.'

Helen approached from behind, but as soon as the child felt the scissors on his hair, he began to struggle and thrash about.

'It usually takes three of us to do this,' Helen gasped. Julian screamed and sobbed. Tim had to lay his whole weight on top of him. Helen cut off a bit of Tim's front hair by mistake, and darted in on Julian's golden curls where she could.

It was dangerous, but it was funny. Tim and Helen were laughing through Julian's howls.

'Done!' she cried. Tim let the child go, and he leaped away and careered round the room, fluttering his hands and looking beautiful enough, with his pale, rosy-lipped face and bouncing golden curls, to break your heart.

His joy, if that was what it was, if he could know joy, propelled him into odd, erratic ballet leaps. Into one corner, touch and lick the wall, then spring backwards, land in a crouch, and launch off in another direction, stiff fingers stabbing the air.

'Thanks for helping,' Helen said in her brisk, practical way. Flushed and dishevelled, his shirt pulled half out of his trousers, Tim put his arms round her and kissed her. Her pale eyes opened wide. Her mouth was still closed when Julian cannoned into their legs and knocked them both off balance against the table.

It was an unsatisfactory kiss, but it was a kiss. He had tasted her mouth. Their bodies had been pressed together. Afterwards, Tim felt a bit turned on. He had taken her by surprise. He had taken her by storm. At home, he began to think about himself as a conquering chieftain. Not a young man kissing a woman older than him; that was not enough. Great scenes must be played out at higher levels, like Shakespeare.

After Kathy, he had thought he was through with sex. Had hoped? Had feared? Now it seemed this might not be so after all.

Witness the dream.

As he struggled up out of a deep, perturbing sleep, the radio alarm brought him a plummy, self-satisfied man signing off after the news programme. Cripes – eight thirty! Tim sat upright. Hang on, it's your day off. He sank back as the beloved, burry voice told him, 'I'm Meery Gordon and I'll be with you for the rest of the day,' soothing as a bedside nurse.

There had been voices in the unfathomable dream, moving water and voices under water.

Dreams could tell you things, as long as you knew how to interpret them. After coffee and buns, Tim interpreted the dream as a suggestion to follow Mary's voice. 'I'll be with you for the rest of the day' meant she would be reading news and announcing the programmes.

He took the radio in the yellow car, and heard her from time to time through the static. While he was back in the flat for a cheese and mustard pickle sandwich, the phone rang, and he turned the radio down low.

It was his mother, wanting to chat about nothing much. A radio quiz was winding down, and Tim wanted to turn up the sound to hear Mary Gordon with the news, so he said, 'I've got to go, Mum.'

Quite soon, Valerie called. It was her half day at the play school and she stopped at her mother's on the way home.

'What's up, Tim?'

'Nothing, why?'

'Mum was worried about you.'

Families. You couldn't *move*.

'You coming round?' Val sharpened her voice.

'No.'

'You used to always come round on your day off.'

'I'm busy.'

'Tim, what are you up to? You sound strange.'

94

'I'm making bombs. Leave me alone, Val.'

'It's a pleasure. What shall I tell Mum?'

'I'll come,' he said heavily.

Mary Gordon would be leaving Broadcasting House when the late afternoon news programme started. Tim stopped in to see his mother and eat cake on his way to the station, where he locked the radio in the boot, which was the only part of the car that locked, and took a train to London.

Outside the great main doors of Broadcasting House, a small group of people were waiting: autograph hunters and a woman with a tired child in a pushchair, the people you saw hanging outside places where the famous came and went, as Tim himself had hung about occasionally.

A man was waiting to see an actress who was being interviewed. 'Who are you here for?' he asked Tim. His teeth were bathed in spit. He was too eager, too avid, with glittering eyes.

'I'm meeting Mary Gordon,' Tim said.

'You mean, you *know* her?'

'Yes.'

'Get away. Why don't you wait inside?'

'Too hot.'

The man told his wife. They muttered together over the push-chair, and looked at Tim.

So when Mary Gordon finally came out, fresh and smiling as if she had not spent all day in a windowless studio, Tim could not just ask for her autograph, as he had planned. He stepped forward and swallowed and said, 'Hello, Mary.'

'Oh,' she said, 'hello.' She turned her full beam on him for a moment, and was gone on slim and nippy legs down Regent Street.

'Oi, oi,' said the man with the teeth. 'She don't want to know, eh?'

'We – we can't be seen together,' Tim said, without much hope of being believed.

He followed Mary at a distance towards Oxford Circus station. Seeing her had been lovely. A look, a smile, 'Hello'. Quite satisfying.

If only ordinary love could be so easy! Romantic fantasies were better than reality. And I can break free any time and be myself, he thought, in the crowded actuality of the tube platform, with the wind of the dragon train's breath preceding it out of the tunnel. This is myself, getting pushed, pushing. A body hanging from one hand, my armpit in the chinaman's face.

Who is myself?

The police had contacted C.P. Games to see whether Tim's story was true. He might have thought of that, but it was a surprise when the play-by-mail company wrote to him, telling him that he was barred from any more games, since false publicity about incitement to violence was the last thing they needed.

'What about my last payment?' Tim wrote back. 'You owe me one pound sixty. And what are you going to do with Blch?'

'He's in a bad spot anyway,' Kevin Sills wrote back, enclosing a postal order. 'He'll have to be eliminated.'

He's mine, you can't do that, Tim thought, but did not write.

Blch could never be eliminated from the consciousness of the universe. The wandering minstrel, teller of tales and fearless warlord of the faithful, lived on in Tim.

It was a restless time, in June. The fair sky beyond the big windows of the second floor, to which customers took colours to match them in daylight, was beckoning and unattainable. Evenings were long and soft, but what to do with them? Tim did not sign himself in on the ushers' rota sheet at the theatre quite so often. They were doing *The Importance of Being Earnest* for two weeks, and he did not think it was funny, although Craig was making quite a hit as second lead.

He asked Tim about the police, some time after that early morning interview.

'I had to report it,' Craig said. 'I hope you understand.'

'Well, it was a bit of a –'

'How did it go?'

'They were extremely interested.'

96

'It didn't get into the papers,' Craig said dismissively.

'Most of the true stuff doesn't.'

'You still play those funny games, Tim?'

'Sometimes.'

'Evil friars. Dungeons and dragons. Demons . . . you know why they're so popular now?'

Tim shook his head. Since he had been expelled from *Domain of the Undead*, he didn't want to talk about it.

'Because the Church doesn't preach about devils and hell any more. But they're in us, Tim, they're in us all, clamouring to get out.'

Buttercup's new gears seemed to have given her vitality all over, plus the fact that good old Jack had tinkered with the spark plugs. Tim began to take the car on the motorway again.

He drove west one evening to investigate downland pubs. Now he did not always have to be the peaceful philosopher stuck in the slow lane, except on hills.

As he pulled out to pass a large sealed lorry, like a gaol on wheels, he saw the driver's face in the rear-view mirror, a narrow lantern-jawed face with a Mexican droop moustache, black side-boards and dark eyes with hooded lids, like an eagle.

Beyond him, Tim moved back to the left, because there was nothing ahead of him to pass. Farther on, the same grey lorry came up from behind and passed him, going much too fast in the middle lane.

That was how accidents happened: juggernauts steaming along so fast that if they had to brake, they would jackknife, or plough into other cars. Tim was offended by the driver with the grim moustache and hard eyes. Why didn't the police go after people like that? If they asked Tim, he could tell them how fast the man had been going.

Several miles along the motorway, down a long hill, he saw flashing blue lights far ahead and a long line of red brake lights. He crawled with them past signs signalling roadworks, and finally came to the crash: two crumpled cars at odd angles, police, scattered orange cones, a smashed guard rail and a red van on its side down a short embankment, with its wheels and obscene underparts facing the road.

Next morning, the paper that he picked up on his way in to work had a picture of the fatal crash, which was thought to have been caused by traffic going too fast at a roadworks contraflow. The police had issued a press and radio appeal for witnesses to come forward.

'I saw him very clearly, miles back. I saw his face in the side mirror. A grey lorry it was, with no lettering that I could see. Yes, officer, about seven thirty, it would have been, not far from the Bramwell exit, going west. Yes, tremendous pace – seventy-five, eighty – I saw the driver's face. I'd know him anywhere.'

'Thanks very much, Mr Kendall. You've been a great help. Sergeant, this is Mr Timothy Kendall, who has made a statement.'

'Thank you for coming in. If we may trouble you further, we'd like your attendance at an identity parade.'

A line of five men, no, six. Short men, tall men, two men in anoraks, one in a blue shirt, brown hair, ginger hair, not much hair, a black man. Second from left, the driver's dark hair receded from his narrow forehead. His mouth was set under the moustache. His flinty eyes looked straight into Tim's eyes, and pierced a message into his brain, a message so ominous that Tim turned to the uniformed man beside him and said in terror, 'None of them is the man I saw.'

After he came out of that waking dream, the man's face stayed with him. He saw it behind his closed eyes, glimpsed it in a crowd, saw it from a bus, passing him in a bus going the other way. The high, bald forehead, the moustache, the sideboards, the stony eyes.

The man was a fact. The speeding lorry was a fact, so was the unrelated accident. The rest was fantasy, but there were elements in it that had become *just as real*. Tim had conjured up one of Craig's 'demons in us all'. He was haunted for days by the lorry driver's face.

CHAPTER NINE

❧

Why be haunted by a mythical lorry driver? H. V. Trotman was there in the flesh.

One evening when Tim got off the bus, Harold was leaning against the side of the bus shelter. He pushed his bulky body upright and fell into step beside Tim, padding like a bear.

'Nice to see you,' Tim said hopefully.

'Didn't think you would? After what you done?'

'I've paid you back. What are you talking about?'

'You know what I'm talking about.'

They had reached the house. Harold went with Tim up the path and passed the bay window, peering into the empty front-room, and followed him up the stairs and into the flat when Tim opened the door.

'Thanks for inviting me in, old son.' Harold looked round suspiciously, as if he expected an ambush. 'Going to offer me a beer?'

'Do you want one?'

'No.' Harold lit a cigarette, turned a chair back to front and sat down with his arms on the back of the chair.

Tim sat down opposite him. It was like his interview at Webster's two years ago, when Mr D. had commanded, 'Give an account of yourself.'

'You.' Harold pointed a blunt-ended finger. 'You tried to pin it on me.'

'What are you – what do you mean?'

'The murders. Kev at C.P. Games told me. Tried to pin it on me.'

'How could I?' Tim sat back, wishing he were smoking himself, so that he could do Elyot nonchalantly tapping off the ash, from *Private Lives*. 'That's ridiculous.' He could not explain why he had borrowed Black Monk for Barry McCarthy. By this time, he was not sure himself. 'They got the man who killed all those people. He was dead.'

'You ... tried ... to ... pin ... it ... on ... me,' Harold droned. Sometimes he sounded like Gareth and Sean.

'I didn't. Suppose I had,' Tim said, avoiding his bloodshot eyes, 'what do you want me to do about it?'

'Nothing. It's what I'm going to do.'

'What –' Tim thought about the royal family, with their necks on the block at the Tower of London. 'What are you going to do?'

'Ah, that's the question, old son.' Harold lifted a finger to the side of his nose. One of the long gingery hairs that grew out of the middle of it waved in the small updraught and curled over the finger. 'You'll have to see, won't you?'

'Please don't threaten me.' Tim smiled ingratiatingly, like a puppy on its back, waggling its paws.

'I'm not threatening you, son.' Harold was a great conversationalist. 'I'm just telling you.'

He left in quite an amicable way, so that Tim thought that was the end of that. Just Harold venting his aggressive feelings, to avoid cancer.

A few days later, Tim stopped Buttercup at a traffic light. A white car drew up beside him. Harold was driving it, looking straight ahead. When the lights changed, he got away fast and cut over in front of Tim, then slowed, so that Tim had to brake, and a woman behind nearly had a heart attack.

Harold continued to turn up now and again in odd places. Tim took to new routes and new habits to avoid him. Sometimes he saw Harold. Sometimes he only thought he did. Sometimes Harold's broad, suffused face and the lorry driver's long pale face were mixed up together in his imaginings.

Several times, the phone rang, and there was no one there.

'Hello ... hello ...' Tim had to answer, because his father was not well ('Always belittled my cough, now perhaps you'll believe me'), and it might be his mother.

Harold disappeared for a time, but then he turned up in Fabrics and Soft Furnishings, wearing clean khaki trousers and a jazzy shirt.

'Yes, sir, can I help you?' Tim said politely, because Mr D. was near by.

'I'm a customer.'

'What is it you want?'

'You know what I want.' Anyone could have written Harold's repetitious dialogue for him.

'Look.' Tim dropped his voice. 'I'll get one of the other assistants to help you.'

'I want to see some of that lot there.' Harold jerked his head at the striped polished cottons, and he and Tim moved over to them.

'Please,' Tim said, his eyes on Mr D. 'Don't do this to me.'

'Got to keep an eye on you, haven't I? After what you done.'

'Harold,' Tim said desperately, 'you've got to get this through your head. I haven't done anything to you.'

'That's what they all say.'

'You're paranoid,' Tim whispered.

'Of course I am,' Harold said loudly. 'Oo wouldn't be? I'll take three metres of that pink and chocolate stuff there.'

And he did. The sale was completed normally and he took the striped cotton away. Actually, it would look quite nice on the woman with the violet mouth.

They were doing *Pygmalion* at the Boathouse. Craig's part was Freddy Eynsford Hill. Tim was there every night. He watched the play from the usher's tip-up seat at the side, and began to have most of Freddy's lines off by heart. He had always been good at memorizing. At school, when he was quite young, they had been amazed at how much he learned, until they were even more amazed to find that he did not understand what most of it meant.

'I spend most of my nights here. It's the only place where I'm happy. Dont laugh at me, Miss Doolittle,' he recited, as he took the long walk home through the quiet streets. If Craig were taken ill, Tim could step in as understudy.

One night, after he had locked the fire doors and tidied up, he walked across the empty car park with Joan, the other usher, who had left her car in the far corner.

Joan's car was there, and another, a white Escort. Harold sat in it. Tim saw his face in the brief flicker of his cigarette lighter.

'I say, Joan,' Tim said quickly. 'My ankle's still bad where I twisted it on the balcony stairs. Do you think you – could you possibly give me a lift home?'

He got into Joan's Mini. The engine of the white Escort started.

'Why do you keep looking behind us?' Joan asked, as she drove him home.

'Oh, I – I thought I saw someone I knew. My brother, as a matter of fact.' Tim could never resist the compulsion to complicate a neat, clean lie with an extra one for decoration.

The white car was not following them.

Julian was back for the holidays, and Helen had a bit of help at home, and could take him to a special day-centre two or three days a week.

On a day off, when it was actually not raining, Tim hired a small motorboat and took them both on the river. Julian wore an orange lifejacket, and Helen kept a close watch on him, while Tim piloted the boat. At the lock, he had to manage the ropes as well, because Helen could not let go of Julian, but he and Zara had often been on the river, and he was glad to show off his competence.

As they chugged slowly upstream, past the wet meadows and the dormant fishermen, Julian was fascinated by the movement of the water against the sides of the boat. Helen held on to the back of his lifejacket while he leaned over and watched the changing shape and flow of the ripples, and reached down to try and touch the glitter of the sun.

It was a beautiful hot day. Helen did not wear shorts or a swimsuit like other women passing by in boats, which perhaps was just as well. She wore a flowered shirt, open to show the knobs where her ribs joined her breastbone, and a long, loose cotton skirt and flat sandals. She had twisted a scarf into a band to wear round her hair. She looked quite nice, like a peasant woman on a barge, calmly watching the life of the river go by.

The dark masses of the trees crowded down the hilly banks to drop heavily leafed branches over the water's edge. The blue sky and small clouds were as clean as the beginning of the world. Tim was peaceful, sitting at the wheel in a dark-blue top and white jeans and pale bare feet. He felt very relaxed and at ease after all last week's disturbances and anxieties. Harold had no place here, and the whole saga of the police visit and the lorry driver seemed to be part of ancient history.

When they tied up by the bank, Helen let Julian lean right over and put his hands in the water. He paddled them about for a long time and fought, with his adventurous tongue already out, to go further down and taste the river.

Tim held him while Helen unpacked the lunch. She had brought a half-bottle of wine and cold sausages and tomatoes and fruit and sandwiches which Julian picked apart to eat the cheese inside. He threw a lot of food in the river. Soon ducks appeared alongside, and down on the stream, like the fairy queen's barges, two swans sailed in to claim their rights.

'Look, Helen, Julian – look! The mother's carrying her babies.'

Inside the curved shelter of the swan's wings, two mouse-coloured cygnets rode on her broad downy back, heads peering this way and that through the feathers, smug in their occupation of the most comfortable place in all the world.

'Look, Julian.' Tim turned the boy's head to make him look, and the boy shook it loose and bit his hand. The cygnets plopped off into the water, as the two swans began to bully and grab at the bread. When Julian waved his arms about, one of them hissed with its great orange beak and raised its powerful wings. Julian shrieked and jumped to the opposite seat, lost his footing, and would have gone over the side between the boat and the bank, if Helen had not grabbed him with the speed and precision of long practice.

After lunch, Tim unmoored the boat and they cruised back down-river. Julian was jumpy, so Tim started to make up a story about the secret life of swans. There was no way of knowing whether Julian understood any of it, or even listened, but Tim enjoyed telling it. The boy, whose skin was a browner version of his golden hair in these early summer days, stared from the other side of the boat, but he could have been staring at the moving tow-path scene behind Tim's shoulder.

He licked the food taste on his hands, and then he moved across to sit behind Tim, hanging an arm over the side to trail his hand in the water.

'The prince could see the beauty of the swan above the water, but under the surface, down in the muddy depths, the engine of the great webbed feet was a secret known only to the tadpoles and fishes. Like you, Julian. Beautiful outside. Inside, a secret we don't know.'

Julian had laid his head against Tim's back.

'He can feel the vibration of your voice,' Helen said.

The child stayed still for a while, fascinated with the movement of the water against his fingers, until he suddenly jerked up his hand and sloshed it across the back of Tim's head.

A narrow boat was going by upstream, with people eating and drinking in the stern well, and children on the roof, and a line of washing. Tim shook the water out of his hair, and Julian celebrated with his strange whoops and hoots. The people on the barge all turned to look. The children pointed.

'I've always wanted to go on a barge trip,' Helen said. 'Without Julian.'

'We went on a barge holiday in Holland,' Tim lied, 'when I was a child.'

Their family holidays had been at Butlins, or on a caravan site, or in a Welsh cottage exposed to north-western gales. Never abroad, because Tim's father did not trust it. When everyone started to go to one Costa or another, he mistrusted not only Spain, but those who went there.

As suddenly as he did everything else, Julian fell heavily across Helen, and was asleep.

'In Holland?' Helen murmured.

'No, actually.' Tim backtracked, before she could ask him about windmills. 'Here, on the river. My sister and I went up to Oxford for a day trip.'

Helen said, with closed eyes, 'This is more fun.'

Just before the last lock, Tim nosed into the bank again, and Helen got out a cake and a thermos of tea. When Tim moved to jump on to the bank and tie up the boat, Julian started to come slowly awake. While Helen was looking for the sugar, he suddenly became completely awake, stood up on the seat and pitched forward over the stern of the boat, arms outspread, into the river.

He surfaced, coughing and spitting, his curls plastered over his astonished eyes, already beginning to float away in his lifejacket on the current. Without a second's thought, Tim jumped in to save him.

Tim was not a good swimmer. He trod water, trying to get his bearings, and saw Julian swimming quite strongly against the stream back to the boat, where Helen bent over the side and hauled him on board.

The gap between Tim and the boat was wider. Don't panic. He swam, with a desperate breast stroke, keeping his face out of the water, and just managed to struggle back to the boat. Helen hauled him in too. She was very strong, for a small woman.

'Julian has swimming lessons,' she told Tim, and laughed. 'Perhaps you should too.'

She dried Julian off and dressed him in the spare clothes she had to take everywhere with him. In the lock, the lock-keeper and the people in the other boats and at the top of the wall could see that Tim was soaking wet, as he jumped off to loop the bow rope round a bollard.

The man at the boatyard said, 'Nice day for a dip, eh?'

When Tim dropped Helen at her flat, she made him come upstairs to be dried off. He put a towel round his waist and sat by the electric fire, keeping an eye on Julian, while Helen took his clothes down to the tumble drier in the basement.

Julian messed himself. While Helen had him in the bath, he began to get sleepy again.

'You won't need your pills tonight, will you, love?' Helen said.

Tim helped to dry him, loving his young, promising body, so cruelly kept from the fullness of life by the damaged brain. Helen put on a fearsome package of nappies and plastic pants, and Tim carried him, asleep, into his little bedroom which was bare of toys or pictures or anything to do damage with or destroy.

Helen went downstairs to get Tim's clothes out of the drier. When she came back with the bundle in her arms, Tim walked towards her and she dropped the bundle and they put their arms round each other and kissed. A proper kiss this time, with all the trimmings.

Helen was very direct. 'Come into the bedroom, if you like.'

In bed, she was under the covers, so Tim could not see what her body looked like, but it felt wonderful, like a woman, like Kathy, who was the only other woman with whom he had ever lain down naked.

'Helen – is it all right if we –?'

'If you want,' she said, and, knowing that he was nervous, 'don't hurry. It's all right, we'll be all right.'

Blch, give me power, Blch be here, ravisher of maidens, be with me.

It was working out all right. He had rolled on top of Helen's calm body when a thud and a piercing shriek came from the other bedroom. Tim rolled off and Helen rolled out and scrambled into Julian's room.

'He fell out of bed.'

By the time she came back, Tim knew that it was not all right. Blch had retreated. Tim turned his head on the pillow and put an arm over his face.

Helen sat on the bed in a dressing-gown that had seen better days.

'It's all right,' she said. 'Oh, I am sorry. After you gave us such a lovely day, and were such a hero, jumping in to rescue Julian.'

Was this why she had let him into her bed?

'Don't worry.' She lifted his arm away from his face and ran her finger along the inside of it. Nothing. It felt like . . . like someone running a finger down the inside of your arm.

'You can come back, you know, any time you like.'

'Not when Julian's here. How did you ever, sort of – do it with your husband?'

'Hardly ever. Julian was only at Val's play school, then, and not away at school. If he wasn't sleepy at night, you couldn't put him to bed, and in those days, I didn't believe in sedatives. That was part of the problem.'

CHAPTER TEN

❧

It was so awful, that Tim put it out of his head, which was what he did with things that were too painful. Helen rang up once. Tim was polite, but not encouraging, since she had obviously rung up only because she was sorry for him. If she was feeling superior because he was too young and too futile and flabby, she was welcome to feel that on her own, with no help from Tim.

When she rang, she did not say anything for a moment, and Tim thought it was Harold, and almost rang off; but she said in her clipped way, 'Is that Tim?', and he said, 'Hello, Helen,' coolly, as if they had never lain in bed and whispered together.

He wished he were still doing play-by-mail, or even role-playing games with Gareth and his moronic mates. It would be a good time to immerse himself in that old seductive world again. He bought another Willard Freeman book, *Star Chasm*, but now that 'All the best, Bill' was not a special hero any more, the discovery game seemed rather childish, and it was too much trouble to keep turning pages forward and back: 'Turn to 122 . . . Got ya! You have slipped into an unfathomable black tunnel with a morass full of writhing hellgrammites at the bottom.'

He put it in the drawer with *Pocket Pickups*, whose advice was based on the assumption that girls were longing for it, so don't hold back. It did not tell you what to do if you had nothing to hold back.

Tim still got a games-playing magazine, because he had taken out a subscription, so he read it out of habit and to keep his mind on ego-boosting topics. It was inevitable that his eye would be caught by the half-page advertisement:

DISCOVER THE REAL YOU! Learn to live rough and fend for yourself. ENTERPRISE Ltd still has a few openings for our adventure training weekend courses that will teach YOU navigation, abseiling, caving, fire and shelter building in the forest.

With no previous experience, YOU can learn to live at one with the Great Outdoors, and go home feeling great. APPLY NOW! The arts of survival could save your life – or someone else's.

This was for Tim. Here comes the great expert in river rescue. He cut out the advertisement and pinned it up over the sink.

Harold had stayed away for three days, five days, a week. Perhaps he was getting tired of his imaginary grievances at last, and would give all his energies to hod carrying.

At the theatre, Tim continued to watch *Pygmalion* almost every night, and to dream that he could be Craig's understudy. Craig did not look all that well. Halfway through the season, he was tired and fed up with the long hours and hard work of repertory.

'I'm sick of this stupid part,' he said to Tim.

I'll have it, if you don't want it.

'Shaw put nothing into Freddy. He's not supposed to have any character. You love the theatre, Tim, but I tell you, don't ever dream about being on the stage.'

Tim remembered when he had recited the murderer's speech: 'I loved her, do you understand?' and Craig had said, 'You should have done the part instead of me.'

'But, Craig, I'll never forget you said, ages ago when I first knew you, you said I ought to be an actor.'

'Did I?' Craig frowned. 'I don't think I did.'

'Oh yes, I'll never forget. You said.'

The Enterprise advertisement over the sink drew Tim powerfully. He polished the taps while he read and re-read its promise of adventure and manhood. The cost for two days was not enormous. No room charge, because you slept under the stars. In a forest!

Tim's mind had pitched camp many times with Blch and his followers, telling tales round the fire where the plump urbok roasted, lying in the bracken, wrapped in his elven-spun cloak, listening to prowling monsters and the eerie night birds' cries.

One evening, he picked up the phone and called Enterprise. Courses were pretty booked up, a man called Steve said, but there were a few openings in three weeks' time.

'Oh – thanks. I'll let you know.'

'Better book now, to be sure of places.'

Do it, Tim, do it. 'All right.' He gave his name and address.

'Are you a pair, or a group?'

Panic. Obviously no one went alone. 'I'm coming with a friend.' Tim's mind was working rapidly. Craig wasn't in the play that week. He had slaved so hard, surely he could get the weekend off. They would share a tent, and talk far into the night in the rustling forest. They would work side by side. It would be much more fun with Craig.

He gave Craig's name, and sent off the fees.

In his lunch hour, he took the advertisement down to the theatre, where they were rehearsing next week's play. Craig was at the back of the theatre, studying his part. Tim sat down next to him.

'Here, look at this.'

'Sounds fun.' Craig read the advertisement. 'Why have people got this craze for survival all of a sudden?'

'You got me there,' Tim said. He had not thought about it. 'To be ready for the nuclear holocaust?'

'Everybody dead but you?'

'I'll be king.'

Craig laughed silently. The theatre was so small, they were quite near the stage, and had to talk in whispers.

'I'm going to have a go,' Tim said. 'Three weeks from Saturday. Look – er, look, it's *Stranger in the Dark* that week. You're not in that. Come with me. Ask them for the weekend off.'

'This management? You must be joking. No, count me out. Too rugged for me anyway.'

*

But not for Tim. He began to set his radio alarm early, and crossed the road to go jogging in the park. Brian and Jack made jokes about it, but he jogged with them some mornings, keeping a few paces behind so that they would not hear him puffing. If he had a heart attack, would they notice, and turn back?

'Getting in training to climb a mountain with us?' Jack wanted to know. 'We're doing the Cuillins if the clear weather holds.'

'I'm into survival,' Tim said.

'Just what you need in Webster's. Thought any more about the management course?'

'No, I mean a proper survival course. Abseiling down rocks, and caves and that.'

'Good boy, good for you.' When Brian smiled, his teeth looked out of his beard like a row of little creatures in the forest undergrowth.

One morning, Tim spotted Harold ahead of them, in his Super-hod boots and baggy cords tied at the ankles, walking with his hands in his pockets along a path at the end of the park.

'Isn't that your friend with the clumsy feet?' Brian asked over his shoulder.

'No.' Tim dropped to a walk, not wanting to get any closer to Harold. 'Got to turn back now. See – see you!' But they had run on in front, already out of hearing.

Tim put off ringing Enterprise, as he put off all difficult phone calls. He left it to the last moment to tell Steve, 'My friend can't come. Illness in the family.'

'I'm sorry to hear that.' The country voice was strong and steady as befitted 'Staff with natural leadership qualities'.

'So, if you could re-pay his fee . . .'

'Well, that's a bit awkward, you see, because it's too late to fill his place.'

'Oh, well, it doesn't matter,' said Tim Kendall, millionaire. He could not make a fuss about the money, and arrive there on Saturday morning with them already hating him. 'Forget it.'

'I wonder if . . . look, I don't know you yet, but you want to do survival, so you must be OK. I wonder what you'd think about giving the place to a very worthwhile young lad who desperately wants to do the basic course, but can't afford it?'

Sod that, was Tim's first instinct. If he's poor, he probably gets more than I do, from the government. But here was a golden chance to show up for a weekend with a built-in fantastic image that would offset any of the horrible mistakes he would probably make on the course.

'I don't mind.'

'Oh, thanks. Norm will be thrilled. Norman Driver. I know him through a school where I've been teaching PE. That's marvellous of you.'

'It's OK.'

That's right, Tim. Chuck your money away. He disliked Norman Driver already.

He disliked him even more when he saw him.

In the car park at the top of the hill where they all met, Norman stuck out like a loose thread from the assortment of young men in their twenties and teens, some of them pretty rough-looking, with dirty hair and spooky clothes, who joked and smoked and pushed each other about, and made Tim feel, as he often felt, like an insecure outsider.

Norman was long and loose-jointed and wobbly, with a hanging jaw and sulky eyes under clean hair cut like a thatch. Steve and Don, quiet, friendly men, shepherding the disorderly group with harmless jokes they had obviously made before, were handing out the giant backpacks and all the gear necessary to survive two days and a night on the wild western hills. Norman had brought a lot of extra junk. He could not get everything to fit into the rucksack. He sat on the ground with legs stuck out and huge boots turned over sideways, and Tim heard him whining, 'Why won't someone help me?' and 'Wish I hadn't come.'

Ungrateful nerd. But Tim could not expect gratitude from him, because he had asked Steve to keep it secret. That added something to the drama of the situation, for Tim. A secret benefactor, Old Money Bags, doing good by stealth.

'He'll just know you as Tim,' Steve had said.

'Well . . .' Tim liked the idea of being incognito. 'Actually, I'm always called – er, Julian.'

'A nickname?'

'Sort of.' He would be the secret prince.

As the prince packed up the bewildering collection of things vital to survival – mess tin, water bottle, poncho, torch, whistle, knife, first-aid kit, plastic bag of dried food and snacks and the extra clothes he had been told to bring – he watched the eight or ten other people from the shelter of Buttercup's rounded flank. All men, except for a short tubby woman in stiff new fatigues from the US Army Surplus, who was there with her big teddy-bear husband, older than the other men, also in a stiff green outfit and shiny new boots.

Some of the others, like Steve and Don, wore Army Surplus, but it was suitably worn and limp. One of the teenagers was in greasy leather, with a belt buckle like metal fangs. His pals wore black T-shirts with the sleeves torn raggedly out and old men's waistcoats gaping open on their bony chests. Thank God Tim had had the sense to wear his crummiest jeans and Jack's cracked old climbing boots with string laces.

Norman's bib overalls and silly red and white striped shirt looked too clean and new. So much for not being able to afford the course.

'Load up, all you lot, and get used to the weight.' Steve stopped being a jokey sheepdog and became a serious natural leader.

They put on the heavy backpacks, with the vinyl sleeping mats rolled on top. Norman put his on kneeling down and could not get up: 'Someone help me!' Teddy Bear's wife staggered to a fence post and leaned her pack on the top rail.

'Listen to me,' Steve told them, 'and go on listening for two days. Listen to instructions, and do as you're told. That's where survival begins, right? Right.'

Tim tried to look intelligent and willing. Norman had stopped listening already. He was gazing vaguely out over the view of rounded green hills and looping hedges, his head tilted on one side to the birdsong. A thin line of saliva hung from the lower corner of the open pocket of his mouth.

'Right, now many of you are strangers, but I want you all to get along with each other. Treat everybody as a friend, and they'll be friendly to you, right?' The overburdened group eyed each other suspiciously. 'Right. Now, let go of the rucksack straps and take the weight on your shoulders. That's where it's going to be for the next hour or two.'

Groans and vomit noises from the boy in leather, whose jacket was armoured in studs and badges and chain links.

'Shake hands with the people on either side –'

'With 'im?' Leather's friend moved away.

'– And tell each other your names.'

It was like in church. Tim had taken his mother to a service a few weeks ago, and nearly died when the overdressed woman next to him put her hand on his arm and commanded, 'Peace.'

'Julian? Hello.' Teddy Bear's wife's name was Janice. Her plump little paw put itself into Tim's hand like a child's. 'What am I doing here?' she giggled. 'I'll be awful.'

'Help each other.' Steve was ending his lecture. He reached for his backpack, which was bigger than anyone's, and swung it easily up over his shoulders. 'Don't give up on anybody. Trust each other. If we were really in a critical survival situation, that could be what saves you.'

'You'll be great,' Tim-Julian told Janice, with a trusty smile.

'Come on then, gang, we're going for a little gentle stroll.'

'Ho ho,' said Chip, the boy with the cropped head that had a scar on it, who had been on the course before. Why would anyone come again, once they knew the weight they would have to carry?

They followed Steve into the trees and immediately plunged down a narrow rocky ravine, where Jack's boots slithered and stumbled as Tim tried to keep his balance, the weight on his back threatening to pitch him into the gorge.

Janice and her husband were behind him, with Don. 'OK?' Don kept asking Janice, and she gasped, 'OK,' and caught her breath, as if she wasn't. Tim could not turn round to look.

At the bottom of the ravine, the leaders went fast along the muddy level and then started to climb a perilous path, where some of the rocks were so big, you had to take a giant step and haul yourself up by clutching bushes and tufts of grass.

There was a muffled cry from behind Tim.

'Hey up, everybody!' Don called out.

They stopped and looked down. Janice had collapsed face forward against the rocky slope, her backpack overwhelming her like a giant turtle shell.

Don helped her to get it off. Teddy Bear said, 'I'll carry it, dear,' uncertainly, and was relieved when Janice said, 'You?', laughing breathlessly up at him. 'It's all you can do to get *yourself* up there, let alone carry two packs.'

'I'll carry it,' Tim said.

Teddy passed Janice's pack up to him, and he toiled on upward with the extra load over his arm.

'Well done, Julian,' Steve called down from far above, a mountain goat poised on a crag. 'That's what I meant. Help the other person. You may need them to help you.'

'In which case, God help you,' Janice panted, climbing the hill behind Tim on hands and knees.

Somehow he struggled on upwards. His back was breaking. His right arm was an agonizing lump of lead. I'll never make it. I'll die here. They'll have to carry my body out of the gorge. He breathed raw hot gases, like a fire-eater.

'You OK?' People looked back from time to time. 'Want any help?'

Tim shook his head, sweating, dribbling out of his gasping mouth.

Good old Tim, they were all thinking – that is, good old Julian. Little guy, but strong as an ox. He would die rather than give in.

On the grassy clearing at the top, Tim dropped the extra pack on the ground, and sat down with his back against it, looking away from the others, so that they would not see his death throes.

'I'll carry it down.' Janice had arrived at the top, red-faced, short curly hair sticking wetly to her round head.

'No, you don't.' Chip grabbed her backpack and started down the hill with it.

'Don't treat me like a woman!' Janice yelled after him into the gorge. The trees grew out of the rocks at odd angles, their roots clawing the air, and you could look down on the dense leaf-mass of their tops, as if you were an eagle, skimming the chasm.

With only half the burden, Tim dropped down more easily to the cool floor of the gorge, where a tiny secret stream found its way silently among dark wet undergrowth that never saw the sun.

'Anyone know where we are?' someone asked.

'Not a clue,' Chip said.

Disappeared off the face of the earth. Unfindable. Two whole days with no fear of Harold! I love this, Tim thought. I love it. I want to come every weekend.

Map-reading and compass lessons in an old barn at the end of the gorge were a bit boring and complicated. Tim made an attempt to understand it in terms of play-by-mail games, but he might have dropped off completely if Norman was not already doing that, his loose eyelids closed and his bristly pale lashes like a toothbrush on his cheek.

Now that they knew how to take bearings and divide the grid of the ordnance map into tiny squares – at least Tim thought that was what they had learned – they were sent off by Steve and Don to find their own way over a ridge of small hills to the caves.

'You may never see us again.' Chip walked off, whistling. He was threatening to look at, with his scarred shaved head and his hatchet face and sharp body. If you met him in an alley on a dark night, you might think twice, but out here, he was just like everybody else. When his Hell's Angels mate had taken off his jacket and stuffed it into his pack as carelessly as if it were not a symbolic breastplate, he was young and skinny and more or less normal too, with the inoffensive name of Eddie.

Tim, who avoided trouble in the town, reorganized his life style as they walked on the short turf towards the hills. He would talk to punks and skinheads on the streets, and make friends with them, discover the human being within the monster: a one-man crusade through the steamier parts of town where the police never set foot.

Norman tagged along at the back of the group. Tim pretended to study the map and compass with the others when they paused to consult.

'Where are we?'

Norman saw a spire. 'Winchester cathedral.' He lived in Winchester. No one paid any attention to him.

When they finally found the entrance to the caves, which was only a narrow crack in the dark rock rising out of the ground, Steve and Don were there before them, brewing up.

Brewing up was lighting a tin of solid fuel, like Vaseline, and boiling water and a tea-bag in your mess tin. It tasted awful. It tasted wonderful. It did not taste like tea. It tasted of earth and growing things and the trickle of stream at the bottom of the gorge, and the fumes of the fuel, which burned in the sun with an invisible flame.

Tim's camping pack had a bag of dehydrated food called beef curry and rice. He wanted to reconstitute it and brew it up, but Don said the serious food was for tonight, and they could eat only their snack bars and glucose tablets.

'Blow out, those bags do,' Don said, in his slow careful way. 'Fill you right up. You go into the caves after that, you'll never get through the drainpipe.'

'What's the drainpipe?' Teddy Bear asked.

'Like it sounds.'

'You'll never get through, Bob,' Janice told her husband.

'Watch me.' He was an anxious man, but determined. When asked, as they had all been, why he had wanted to come on this course, he had answered, 'I've got to know that I can make myself do it.'

117

His wife had answered, 'Well, I couldn't let him come without me, could I?'

As it turned out, he did get stuck for a while in the drainpipe, which was a very low and narrow passage through the rocks, deep in the bowels of the earth.

Janice took an easier route with Don and Norman, who had shone the miner's lamp on his helmet into the entrance of the drainpipe and had an attack of the shivers; but Teddy Bear made himself try the pipe.

Tim and the other skinny ones managed to wriggle through. Tim was a troll, a troglodyte, a prehistoric man, terrified of being buried alive in the caves, yet exhilarated to discover that he could slither and scramble, and propel himself through slanting fissures with his shoulders and bootsoles. It was either do that, or be stuck in this cold crypt for ever.

Coming last, Bob had to be pushed from behind and pulled from the front before he popped out of the pipe like a cork, telling himself, 'I did it,' chewing on the words under his grey-black moustache, nodding his head, so that the yellow lamp-beam travelled up and down Eddie's skinny leather legs, caked in clay from the floor of the slippery caves.

Working their way out an hour later towards a slit of light ahead, they had to climb steep, wet rocks under a jagged roof. Coming out into the sudden sunlight, the leaders looked at each other and blinked, a filthy group of miners, surprised by the sky.

Tim took off his hard hat and switched off the lamp, and imagined that he had been down the pit all his life. He was hollow with hunger. Now he would tramp back to a row of blackened cottages, where a pregnant, nagging wife would scrub his back before the fire and feed him with meat pudding.

Some of the miners went down to the stream to get a drink. Tim and the others turned to watch Don and the other two resurrect themselves through the narrow exit in the rocks. At last, muffled thuds and cries brought the top of Norman's hard hat hesitantly into view, like a baby wondering whether it was worth being born.

'Where's Janice?' Bob called to him.

'Stayed back . . . with Don . . . have a rest . . . Oh, help.' Norman raised his helmeted head and the roof banged it down again. 'Got to get out of here.'

His long incompetent fingers clawed at handholds and slipped off. He fell back a few feet and screamed that his ankle was broken.

'I can't get out!' His voice was shrill and hollow, like a reed.

'God, if he panics – 'someone muttered. Steve was down at the stream.

'Help me! Why won't you help me – e – e?'

Tim put on his hard hat and went back into the hole on his stomach, reaching out for Norman. His groping fingers found panicking cold hands, which clutched painfully.

'All right, Norm?' He felt strong and heroic. 'Come on, bend your knee up, find a foothold. I'll pull you.'

'I can't,' Norman gasped. He was limp, a dead weight.

'You can.' Tim moved his head to shine his helmet lamp on the ghastly stricken face. 'You can do it.'

'I'm done for.'

'Shut up, Norman, you can do it. Look at me. Get your light on my face, that's right. Look in my eyes. Look at me. Push with your feet. I've got you, follow me.'

Norman struggled, Tim backed off and pulled him up a foot. His arms were coming out of their sockets. Just when he thought he would let Norman go, someone took hold of his own feet and began to pull him up and back.

'All right, mate? Got yer, mate. Take it easy, Norm. Come on, Julian mate.' They got the boy out of the caves at last. Tim and Chip did, me and my mate, and laid Norman out shivering on the grass like a dying chicken.

'Thanks, mate,' Tim said to Chip.

Norman didn't thank anybody. It wasn't his style.

In the woods where they were to camp for the night, pairs of people would put their ponchos together to make a rough tent over a ridgepole.

'Plenty of dead wood about,' said Don, plodding about in his methodical way to find just the right branch to make his little home with Steve. '*Don't* cut any fresh wood.'

So the next thing seen was poor old Norman struggling to break a healthy, bouncing sapling.

Who was going to pair off with him? Bob and Janice were together, Chip and Eddie. The other boys chose spots to pitch tents, two by two. Tim was left with Norman.

'Make your shelter, then eat,' Don said, but Tim wanted to eat first.

'I'm starving,' he told Norman. He could almost faint at the thought of beef curry and rice.

'I'm not,' Norman said. 'I don't like the look of my shepherd's pie. It's all dried up.'

'It's dehydrated, you jerk. You add water.'

'I don't like shepherd's pie. You jerk too.'

Somehow they got a dry log wedged between two trees, and fixed their ponchos over it. Every time Norman moved about, unpacking his kit, he trod on one side and pulled the whole lot down.

After he had put it up again for the third time, Tim tipped his bag of curry into the mess tin, added water and lit the cooker.

'That looks good.' Norman came along with one of the ropes from the tent trailing round his foot. 'Can I have that?'

'Eat your own.'

'I'll have wind.'

'Not in my tent, you won't.'

Norman sniffed and snuffled. He could not breathe properly through his crooked nose. That was why his fat slug lip hung open. The thought of spending the night with him tempted Tim to wish Norman was still stuck in the caves. Give him something to sniffle about. I ought to have put a mage's evil spell on you, not bust my muscles dragging you out.

After he had messed about with his shepherd's pie, which Tim had to cook up for him, Norman belched loudly several times –

'Wolves howling tonight!' from the next tent – and crawled under the shelter. When he took off his boots, Tim wished he hadn't. Norman lay down in the middle of the tiny tent, forced his long awkward body into his sleeping-bag with groans and an occasional sob, and turned his face to the poncho wall.

Other couples had lit camp fires. Tim prowled about in the wood, moving close to a fire, if invited. Eddie and Chip were having a smutty conversation about a girl Chip had met on a war game weekend. 'Randy as hell, I was. Nothing like shooting people to get you going. Shoot 'em with paint pellets,' he told Tim. 'It's fantastic. Kill! Kill! You'd love it.'

A few people were sitting round the big fire that Steve and Don had built efficiently, listening to stories about other Enterprise weekends. What will they say about me and Norman when we're gone? Tim sat on a log at the edge of the group.

'Done well, you have, Julian.' Steve instantly flashed his way on to Tim's list of specials. 'Like it so far?'

'It's all right.' Tim meant, I love it.

'Coming again?'

'I might.'

'You come again, get to know the ropes, you could give me and Don a hand, with bigger groups, help some of the beginners.'

'All right.' I'd *love* to!

When Tim went back to his poncho home, the most clumsy and rickety of all the shelters, Norman, rolled in his sleeping-bag like a maggot in a cocoon, was still awake.

'Where were you? It's scary in this forest. I heard animals prowling.'

Norman was lying on both the vinyl mats, but Tim said nothing. He did not want to talk.

Norman did. 'Julian,' he said. 'I say, Julian.'

Tim curled up on leaves and bracken, away from him. The shelter was so small that their bodies touched through the sleeping-bags.

'Julian, listen. In that awful cave – why did you tell me to look at your eyes?'

'To give you strength.' Tim turned back to him. 'To calm you down, sort of, and, like, pull you out by magnetism.'

'You a hypnotist, then?'

Why not? Tim could be if he wanted. It was true, he had charmed Norman out of the caves.

'Yes,' he said. 'I am.'

Next morning, after a lecture on berries and nuts and living at one with nature, it was another long tramp to the abseiling cliff.

They came round a corner in an overgrown abandoned quarry, and, God! there it was. A sheer rock face, miles high, thousands of feet high, a hundred and thirty feet high.

'Not going up there,' said Norman.

'That's not the problem,' Chip said. 'It's coming down it.'

Steve had brought abseiling harness and ropes in the van: beautiful, slender, silky ropes, that he uncoiled lovingly, and wound round himself to demonstrate how they could tie a bowline knot one-handed in mid-air. 'Let's see you all do it.'

'Why would we want to?' Bob could not do it.

'If you were in trouble and needed an extra rope thrown down.'

'One rope isn't strong enough, then?'

'Sure. The breaking strain point is six and a half tons. No one's as heavy as that.'

'You should see my Mum,' Eddie offered.

They practised abseiling on the nursery slope, a smaller rock only about thirty feet high. The worst part was stepping backwards into space. Tim dithered on the edge.

'Go on.' Steve was beside him on another rope. 'You'll love it.'

'I want to, but I don't want to.' Tim licked his dry lips. His stomach had already risen up.

'Fear and desire are friends.'

'I don't –' Tim began to say, but Steve said, 'Go!' at the same time, so Tim went.

Sitting in the webbing harness with the rope passing through the clip on the front of the belt, Tim dropped easily down the rock, checked himself by raising the lower part of the rope in his right hand, and pushed off from the rock face to jump the last few feet.

'Nothing to it.'

Janice floated down like a fat pigeon. Even Norman managed fairly well, shouting, 'I don't like it!', but picked himself up at the bottom, and walked off with a silly grin, to brew up, wagging his thatched head.

Teddy Bear was the last to go down. He stood for a long time at the top, asking questions, fiddling with the harness, turning to look down. 'Don't look down!' from Janice and Tim at the bottom. The rope that was tied to a tree with Steve's bowlines had been passed through the clip. Steve showed Bob how to lean back to take the strain. He had one foot over the edge.

'Come *on*,' Janice whispered. The foot went back up. 'Oh, God, if he doesn't do it, he'll be a wreck. He'll hate himself, that's what he's like. Dear God, please make him come over the top.' Janice clutched Tim's arm. 'Please, God, push him or something, you've got to. Make him do it,' she pleaded, and Tim found that he was praying with her.

'Help him, Lord,' breathed Janice, and Teddy Bear was over the edge, hanging like a German sausage on a string, twisting sideways, pulled straight by Steve, dropping down ('Thank *God!*'), landing bumpily and staggering into a bush – but landing.

'We prayed for you,' Janice told him, 'me and Julian.'

It had worked. Perhaps Tim could take up praying, as well as hypnotism.

When Steve said that they were all to abseil down the soaring, sheer rock face, Janice said to Bob, 'Let's not test God too far.' He stayed below and practised bowlines, while she climbed up the rough slope at the back of the cliff, with the others.

'Don't want to do it.' Norman puffed and snuffled and panted at the top of the hill.

'Yes you do.' Hadn't Tim got him out of the caves? Hadn't he prayed Bob down? He could get Norman down the cliff.

'I can't.' Norman shook his head, looking down, horribly far down. Below them, emerging from a fissure high up in the rock, a bird took wing and soared away, to show them it was easy.

'You can do it,' Tim insisted. 'Look at me.' Norman turned his head.

Tim narrowed his eyes and glinted them hypnotically.

'Oh –' Norman swayed about. 'You give me confidence. Perhaps I will.' He hung his lip. 'Perhaps I won't.'

He wanted everyone else to go first. Terrified, Tim leaned back in the harness, heard Steve say, 'Go!', thought, I am going to die, pushed off from the edge, dropped, found the rock with the flat of his feet, and bounced himself off to sail out and down like a bird in a great dizzy swoop. I can fly!

I can fly. He kept on the belt and leg harness and started up the hill again, light-headed, not feeling the effort of the climb, ecstatic.

'Can I go again?'

'Sure.' Steve grinned. 'Just let Norman have his turn.'

Norman was at the edge of the cliff, as dead white as if he really were going to be pushed off, uncontrolled, into space.

Go on, you bugger, Tim thought. You've got this far, and snored all night, and your feet smell, and I've paid for you and all. 'Get going, Norm.'

'Leave him alone,' Steve said. 'He's all right.'

He wasn't. On the rim of the precipice, Norman's long wobbly legs buckled. He knelt there, clutching the taut rope in front of him.

'Get on your feet,' Steve said steadily. 'Lean *back*.'

Norman gibbered. Standing in front of him, Tim tried to force the energy again.

'You *can*, Norman, you can. You can fly like a bird. Lift your head and look at me – you can fly!'

Norman looked up, and reached his arms forward to Tim.

'Lean *back*!' shouted Steve, but Norman's feet dragged over the edge, and his face bumped and scraped against the rock as he went over.

He landed in a heap, covered in blood, and the ant people at the bottom of the quarry ran towards him.

'What the hell?' Steve turned furiously to Tim. 'What the hell were you trying to do? "Look at me – you can fly." You must be crazy.'

'It wasn't my fault.'

'He'd have been fine if you hadn't interfered.' Steve put the second rope through the clip on his belt and disappeared over the edge without looking at Tim again.

Tim went slowly back down the hill the way he had climbed up it. Norman was being cleaned and patched up. Steve was angry and tired. Don would have to drive Norman home, because he could not go by train.

'What happened?' everyone was asking. Norman didn't know, and Steve did not say.

But the general opinion was: Norm should not have been here. So even that was Tim's fault, as well as everything else.

'How did the weekend go?' Brian asked.

'Amazing.' Tim could not tell him about the disaster of Norman, so he boasted a bit about the caving and the abseiling, and the rigours of a night in the small copse that Norman had thought was a forest. 'It was fabulous.'

But the dream of Enterprise was finished and faded like a dawn waking. Back to my real self. Tim hunched gloomily on the window-sill in his flat, and contemplated reality.

Back to Harold.

Tim had not been home more than an hour or two before he heard the heavy tread on the bottom of the stairs. He knew Brian was at home, so he could not refuse to open the door and risk Harold going berserk on the steps.

'Hello – er, hello, friend.'

Steve had lectured them, 'Treat everybody as a friend and they'll be friendly to you.' Might be worth trying.

'Don't give me that.' Harold came in. 'You're no friend of mine, after what you done. Really eats into me, it does, like a cancer, and I won't never be able to forgive you, not in the rest of your life.'

Why hadn't he said, 'Not in the rest of *my* life'? The suggestion that Tim, although younger, was going to die before him was very unsettling.

'I've got some lemonade.' ('Don't give up on anyone.') 'Would you like some?'

'Yer.'

'Something to eat?'

'Yer.'

Harold sat down with his knees apart and his arms on the table, as if he had a knife and fork in his fist, ready to bang the handles for service.

Tim gave him lemonade and some stale bread and the last of the cheese. He was too nervous to eat or drink anything himself.

The situation was horrible. Two days of escape, and then the handcuffs were on again. How was he ever going to break free? Threatening again to report Harold for menace might make him angrier. Actually reporting him might send him right over the top.

And what could Tim really tell the police?

This friend of mine keeps turning up – well, he was a friend, but now I'm afraid of him.

Why is that, Mr Kendall?

He said I'd die before him.

Well, you may have a pink face from two days in the great outdoors, but other than that, you don't look in the best of shape.

It's the eyes, isn't it, constable? Haunted-looking.

When Harold had gone, Tim looked for a long time at his face in the mirror.

Haunted eyes. No wonder he was starting to make mistakes at work. Three times, Mr D. had caught him standing about day-dreaming when customers needed help.

He had read a price ticket wrong on Purbeck moiré, and it had got into the customer's account, and when she came in later for an extra couple of metres, she spotted the mistake and raised hell with Mr D.

'I took full responsibility,' he said stiffly to Tim, 'because it's not my policy to reveal the shortcomings of the staff.'

'Thank, er, thank you, Mr D.'

'Not to protect you.' He stood by the desk with his knuckles on its tidy surface. 'To protect the department. I just want you to know, it's very painful for me.'

'I'm sorry.'

'Sorry is neither here nor there. You want to remain with us, I take it?'

Tim nodded, and stared at the floor.

'Well, then.'

Tim had hardly heard what he said. Sometimes he thought he might be going deaf.

'What are you waiting for, young man? Clear out of here. Clear out and do your duty out there on the floor.'

'Fantastic,' Chip had said to Tim, about the war games. 'Kill! Kill! You'd love it.'

Well, what did Tim have to lose? He could never go back to the survival course, and Warfare sounded much easier. You didn't have to learn anything. You just ran about, going, 'Bang, bang, you're dead,' which would be as good as recapturing childhood. He deserved that. He really deserved a break away from what Val called stress, and he called the jitters.

Stress was fashionable. He had it.

'What do people do for stress, Val?'

'Take a break, if they've got any sense. Let themselves relax. Stop driving themselves.'

'That's something you'll never have to worry about anyway, Timothy,' Colin said. He was getting as nasty as Val. He'd better watch out.

Enterprise had ended up in anticlimax and disappointment because of Norman, but also because there had been no one to tell the tale about the adventures to when he came home. What would it be like if he came back splattered with paint from a day at the war games? No beer in the flat and a tepid shower, because Brian and Jack kept the water temperature low in the summer. He might go home and tell his mother. She would love it, but she would call out, 'Come in here, Wallace, and listen to this,' and Little Hitler would make a meal of it.

Helen wouldn't, though. She would listen and nod, with the parallel frown lines between her small careful eyes, and only interrupt to say things like 'That sounds nice' in rapid little rushes.

'Hullo, Mrs Dyer. I'm, er, I'm sorry to bother you, but I need to talk to Helen. Could you ask her to ring me?'

'She's just come in, as a matter of fact. Her helper's here. I'll run up and get her to come down. Hang on.'

Only a minute to think what he was going to say.

'Tim? Hullo, how nice.' So she was still speaking to him.

'Yes, I, er – when's Julian going to camp?'

'Two middle weeks in August. I can hardly wait. No, forget that. I shouldn't have said it.'

'Yes, you should. Relieves the stress. Talking of that – I say, Helen, I wondered if – suppose you came round to my place then, on a Saturday evening when Julian's away? I could make supper and we could walk across the road and hear the band concert in the park.'

'*If it doesn't rain.*' They said it together, and laughed.

He told her how to get there. 'What time? Well, look, I'll be out all day. Something rather special . . . well – tell you about it when I see you, right?'

'All right.'

Val, Zara, Gail, Lilian, any of the few women he knew would have said, 'Tell me *now*!' (And been disappointed with it if he had.)

'I should be back by six.'

Get a frozen pie, Tim. Thaw it out. Frozen potatoes and peas, thaw them out, cook them quick. Cheese . . . French bread . . . wine. Economize later.

Warfare took place about thirty miles away, partly in a wood, partly in open country on a windy hillside. There were about forty people, some of them women, which Tim had not expected: wives, girl friends, a blonde called Judy with a group from her office, in bright track suits. Some of the men were mates from a pub. They hung about the Army tent and the camp fire, and drank coffee and joked noisily about being hung over and short of sleep from Friday night, looking to see who was impressed.

Derek, who was in charge, kitted everybody out in patchy green and black and brown camouflage overalls. Tim's cammo suit was too big. It bagged and sagged, until the webbing holster belt pulled it in more trimly. He pushed the legs into his white sports socks. When Derek gave him the paint pellet gun and he felt the weight of it, he knew he wouldn't have missed this for anything. The cammo overalls, the heavy black pistol, the thick goggles – he wasn't just Tim, stuffed up stupid with the fourth day of a summer cold. He was anybody he wanted to be, anonymous in the goggled crowd, a soldier.

The staff of Warfare had seemed easy-going, but as soon as they had got everyone out of the tent and out of the little huts labelled MEN and WOMEN, it was different. Now it wasn't Derek with long eyelashes who was in charge. It was Joe, ex-sergeant with laced boots and a tight, strutting bottom and an Army beret flat on his bristled head, and a voice that sobered up the gigglers and hung-overs.

'Right, now you're mine, you lot. Gawd, what a bloody awful lot.' He paced in front of the line of men and women who had paid twenty pounds to be told, 'Let's see you stand up straight and knock off the horse shit.'

Tim squared his shoulders under the loose overalls, and added Sergeant Joe to his list of heroes.

'Right, I've got fifteen minutes to try to teach you what it would take you six weeks to learn in the Army, which is where you'd all be a lot better off now if you had been.'

While he told them the rules of the game and the things they mustn't do and what would happen to them if they did them, they all put on the goggles and the green plastic face mask, which had a nose shield and mouth slits to breathe through, and did nothing for Tim's cold.

Judy and her friends, straggling out of line and looking at the same time more relaxed and more serious than the men, were chewing gum under the face masks.

Joe showed them how to take off the safety catch and fire the pistols. Unloaded, the CO_2 charge made a 'fglop' sound, like a belch. They loaded the paint pellets and fired at a dummy in the middle of the field.

Tim raised his gun, narrowed his eyes behind the goggles and fired – 'Phut!' like an air gun. He had never fired rifles at fairgrounds. This was the first time he had ever fired anything except the toilet plunger at the window. His heart raced. Had he hit the dummy? It was covered with splotches of red paint. One of them could have been his.

'Couldn't hit a haystack, most of you men,' Joe jeered. 'Bull's-eye, all the ladies. Watch 'em. In the woods, every man is a possible rapist. They may aim low.'

Could Tim shoot women? Yes, if they were going to shoot him. Disguised, they didn't look like women now, this lot, except Judy with her froth of bleached hair bursting out above the strap of her goggles.

'You'll be in two teams for the whole day, so you better like each other. Green guards the green flag and tries to get Yellow's flag. Yellow ditto, in reverse. That clear? Even to you lot? ... I said, "That clear?"'

'Yes, Joe.'

Tim and some others said, 'Yes, sarge.'

'Right. Let's have the shoulder flashes, Derek. We'll divide up.'

Here it came. The agony of picking sides, and Tim would be picked last. Or he'd be left out, like he was in the western copse, stuck in a tent with Norman.

Sergeant Joe evened out 'the ladies' and then – Tim's saviour – simply divided the line in two and gave out the shoulder tabs. The line broke up and several people dashed off again through the hedge to the little huts. In a real war, did people keep dropping out to have a pee?

Tim's Green group gathered together to plan. Plan what? 'Pick a leader,' Derek told them. 'Who's played before?'

'I have, as a matter of fact.' Before any of the others could finish saying, 'So have I,' a cocky little chap called Ken had made himself leader and was telling everyone what to do. Some to guard the flag in camp, some to go ahead and attack, some in the middle ground.

Tim was in the middle group, which went off among the trees from their camp in a clearing in the wood.

'Back up the attackers, watch each other, work as a team,' but as soon as the whistle blew, everyone went off on their own, and Tim didn't know where anybody was, and it was wildy exciting and total chaos.

Shots somewhere to the left. Shots to the right, ahead and behind him. Phut – ow! One very close. He saw a yellow shoulder flash low down in the undergrowth and fired, and immediately, like the echo of his own shot, he was hit in the leg.

The red paint looked like blood on his thigh. It hurt. Derek had said it wouldn't hurt, but it did.

If you were hit, you were dead, and you put on an orange vest to show you were out of that game. The game had hardly begun, and he was out of it, like being first out in musical chairs at a children's party, slinking to the wall as the music started again. A mother had sung out, 'Poor old Timmy, why is it always you?' He could hear her now.

He put on the orange dead-man's vest and trudged up the path back to his camp. Sarge was there and one of the other staff, and the Green defenders, crouched by a rough wooden barricade, and behind trees and in overgrown hollows.

First hit! No one said that, but they might as well have. Tim kept his face mask down, although it was hard to breathe. Perhaps he should go home. But out of the trees came another orange vest, then another and another, masks pushed up, a hand up to goggles –

'Goggles down!' from Joe. 'If I have to tell you again, the gate's up there.'

Goggles down. It was cocky Ken, the leader. He had been shot just after Tim. Cheers.

Now it was all right to be dead. They sat on a bank. 'How d'you cop it?' 'Ran right into it.' 'I got one of theirs, though.'

'I got two,' Tim said. Who would know?

Behind the low barricade in the defenders' fort, one of the girls lay on her stomach, gun through a gap in the logs, long black hair down her back. A pioneer woman, she looked, tense against the creeping Indians. Or an Indian squaw, tense against the pioneers. She looked dramatically businesslike, but when she raised her head to see who was coming, she got picked off with a splat of paint on the goggles.

Two of the other defenders had got fed up waiting and gone off. Another was re-loading his gun with a tube of pellets when a Yellow man burst out of the trees, grabbed the green flag off a branch and ran back, just as a Green man dodged out into the clearing with the yellow flag, in time to get shot in the back by the defender of his own side who had finished re-loading.

The dead man dropped the flag. 'You silly sod. Grab the flag!' he yelled to his treacherous murderer, who ran forward, fell over a tree root and was shot by a sniper behind a bush, who picked up the yellow flag and ran.

It was poor old Tubby. His friends from the pub called him that. Moon-faced and cheerful, he had lost his belt as soon as it was given to him, spilled his coffee, fallen in the mud on the way to the camp, and dropped his glasses when he took his goggles off to wipe them. 'Keep those ruddy goggles on, what have I told you!'

'Is that it?'

'Unless one of ours gets the flags back.'

'How many are left?'

'Damn.' A double whistle showed the game was up.

Having watched the Green team make fools of themselves, Sergeant Joe decided to help.

'That was horrible. Who's your leader?' Ken had disappeared. Large steady Dave took over. 'Work as a team,' Joe said. 'Three or four stay in the camp, one go for the flag, and a bunch of others back him up. Cover him. Get killed. One or two try to stay alive to go back with him. He can't do it alone.'

I could, Tim thought. I could run and dodge through the trees like that Yellow bloke did.

'Who'll run?' Dave asked. 'Liz, Judy? Girls are faster, because they don't drink beer.' Liz and Judy shook their heads, chewing. 'Who else is fast?'

Pause, then, 'I am,' Tim said.

'OK.' Dave believed him. 'Give it a go.'

People looked at Tim and smiled and gave him a thumbs up. They were more of a team now, knowing each other's names, beginning to see a dim sort of strategy, all muddy and paint-splashed, all taking it more seriously. Judy tucked her conspicuous hair under a cap. Tim pulled his cammo overalls down over his white socks.

'Pair off,' Joe said. 'Work with an oppo.'

Quickly, they paired off. Tim's oppo was Tubby. Of course. But he was a good enough bloke. He bumbled about, and thought Tim knew what to do.

They prowled through the wood together between shooting on both sides, people being killed, heavy breathing, branches snapping, danger everywhere. Tim's eyes stared like a lynx. His skin stood on end like cat fur. Tubby was wheezing and cursing under his breath, but he followed Tim, good old oppo, as they crawled and dodged and pushed their way through brambles and bracken to the hedge that bounded the enemy camp.

The Green people who had started out to cover Tim had disappeared, dead or lost. Now or never. 'Cover me!' Tim crouched at a gap in the hedge, and ran. Behind him, Tubby fired three wild shots and squealed as he was shot.

Tim ran, weaved, crouched behind a tree, saw the yellow flag on a post, ran out, yelled in a high voice, and got killed within a few yards of his goal, desperate arm flung out.

The Greens improved, and it was two games all at lunchtime:

smoky hamburgers over the oil-drum fire, easy talk, exploits exchanged, jokes, friendly insults. Tim ate three hamburgers. He and Tubby sat together in silence, waiting to get on with the war. Tim had a sinus headache. The frame of Tubby's glasses was broken, where he had jammed the goggles over them crookedly.

Tim hoped to run for the flag again, but after lunch, Mary was chosen, because she had eaten only fruit. Tim and Tubby went with the group that backed her up. They were attacking the camp with the rough log fort. The defence was brilliant. Unseen snipers picked off the Greens one by one, and picked off Mary when she made her dash for the flag.

Tim and Tubby had thrown themselves behind a tree trunk on the bank of a pond. Tubby, goggling through his glasses behind his goggles, took out one of the defenders.

'Did I get him?' He raised his head to see, and got shot in the side of the neck.

'They got me, pal.' He slid backwards down the bank to the pond.

My oppo! The emotion was real, and the tense excitement. Tim was on his own. Imperishable Tohubo, alone against the world! He fired two shots in the direction of the shot that had killed his mate, and realized he was almost out of ammunition. No time to re-load. He scrambled over the tree trunk, and ran for the yellow flag. The young skinny girl was behind the low barricade of the fort. Tim rushed at her, brandishing his pistol, and yelled, 'Drop the gun!'

She did. She lost her nerve. He was too close. Surrender!

With a hoarse cry, Tohubo pulled the flag off the branch, turned, took out the last defender with his last shot, and ran for his own camp as if he had been charging and dodging through woods all his life, his nose and head miraculously cleared, and flung himself, gasping, on the ground by his own flag post.

His team, alive and dead, crowded round him.

'How did you do it?'

'One surrendered, one I took out.' Sitting up, he told the tale, breathless, his chest heaving like an Olympic runner's.

'Good for you,' they said. 'We're ahead now. Good old Tim.'

Tubby turned up with his orange vest askew, and put an arm round Tim's shoulders. 'We did it,' he said. 'I died for you.'

The Warfare games were not finished, but anything else would be an anticlimax. Tim wanted to go home now, in his blood-stained cammo, with his gun: muddy, exhausted, bruised and triumphant conqueror, Tohubo the invincible, Blch the returning hero.

When the others went back to base camp to start the next battle, Tim sneaked off sideways through the trees, crossed a stream and found his way along the side of the wood and through a wire fence to where he had left Buttercup.

At home, he parked the car and got out, hoping Brian or Jack would see him wearing the cammo, disappointed to see through the garage side window that their car was not there. He went slowly up the stairs to give the neighbours a chance, if they were in their garden behind Jack's vegetable plot.

He felt absolutely marvellous. Normal. Real. Rooted on the earth. Light years away from the compulsive fantasies of the police witness and the haunting lorry driver.

When Helen arrived, he was sitting watching the door, with the CO_2 pistol across his lap. She rang the bell. He put the gun under a cushion on the couch bed and opened the door. Helen gasped, and said, 'Oh! You look –'

'War games,' he said crisply.

'Are you hurt?'

'Paint.'

'Was it fun?'

'Terrific.'

She wore a rather dowdy sand-coloured dress, full and long – she had lived with those legs long enough to know what to do about them – and the childish sandals she had worn in the boat.

The oven was heating. The wine was opened. Tim had planned to say, 'Welcome to my place,' but Blch would not let him. Suddenly, the bold warrior rushed in and took charge, and he pushed Helen on to the bed and undid the front of her dress.

'Tim, you're so – wait, you're hurting me.'

Strong in his cammo armour, spattered with blood-paint, Blch had her skirt up and her pants down, even while she said, 'Let me –' and he claimed his rights, as all returning heroes should, and she did not struggle, which was just as well, but let him ravish her.

Afterwards, she stroked the cammo overalls and said comfortably, 'That was what you needed, then.'

'You don't mind?'

'Everybody needs something. With my husband, I used to have to imagine he was Robert Redford.'

'Do you mind this?' Tim pulled the pistol from under the cushion.

'I would have, if I'd known.'

They put the gun under the pillow when they went back to bed after they had heated and eaten the food. They had drunk the whole bottle of wine, and Tim had told Helen she was his oppo.

'Do you want to keep this on?' Helen fingered the cammo.

'I'd better. Do you think I'm daft?'

'I had a boy friend once,' Helen said, 'who went to bed in a great thick belt he'd bought off a market stall, with the buckle made of motorcycle parts.'

'Rather painful.'

'He turned it the other way round.'

She was quite experienced. It was amazing.

❧

This you are not going to believe, Jack would say to Brian. Our life has really been enriched since the day we let the young 'un in upstairs.

Brian had gone off early to see his occasional lover, and Jack was having a late leisurely breakfast outdoors, on the paving at the back. Because Brian was not here, with his stern scruples and cautions, Cindy was sitting outside in a sun dress and dark glasses, large straw hat tied over the blonde hair with a scarf that ran round the crown and through holes in the brim.

Tim's door opened, she would tell Brian, and out came our

likely lad, and behind him – yes, I knew this was a lucky Sunday – a real . . . live . . . woman.

Go on, Brian would say.

No, honest. They looked as if they'd just got out of bed.

Tousled?

No, in good nick. They were both at the top of the stairs. Tim looked round a bit furtively, and his eye lighted on the top of my Ibiza hat. So after she'd gone . . .

No. Better leave the rest of it out.

❧

Tim's eye alighted on the top of a wide straw hat with Brian's girl friend underneath it, at ease on a garden chair, with a mug of coffee and a toasted bun on the little table.

Helen would not let him drive her home. She would take the bus to the cathedral and go to the service at ten thirty.

'Come with me?'

'I don't think so.' Being unofficial tour guide and stigmata expert was one thing. Tim could not sit through a service. 'I'll drive you there.'

'Not if you're not coming in.'

He walked her down the road and waited with her for the bus. They did not say much. You didn't need to with Helen, which was a relief when you had nothing to say.

When he came back, the woman in the sun hat was still in the garden. Feeling bold, Tim walked under the stairs and went round behind the house, and said, 'Lo.'

'Hello.' The woman tilted the hat and smiled up at him with large lips that had lipstick on the outer edge, with a line where it met the uncoloured part inside. The smile was wide and cheery.

'Here – hold on.' Tim took a step backwards. The woman was Jack.

'Sit down, Tim. I'll get you some coffee.'

Speechless, Tim shook his head.

'Come on, sit down while I get it. It won't take a moment.'

Once you knew it was Jack, you knew it was Jack, as it were. The first 'Hello' from under the hat had sounded merely like a woman with a deep voice. Once you knew, the voice was a dead give-away. But if you didn't know, if you were not familiar with Jack's smiling face, you could be taken in.

So if Brian . . . then they were . . . hang on a minute, what about Jack's girl friend Janet Fox in Webster's Accounts Department?

Having given Tim a short break to recover, Jack came back with a mug of coffee. He walked like a man, his muscular legs in white tights.

'Thanks for not minding,' Jack said, disregarding the obvious fact that Tim did mind. 'I put in two sugars, that's right, isn't it? Come on, Tim, take a good look at me, it's all right. You came out here just now believing I was a woman, didn't you? That's really great. And the few times you've seen me before, through the window, I passed, didn't I?'

'Yeah.' Tim looked into his coffee, out over the small lawn to the vegetable garden, down at his hands, which had gone white at the fingertips. 'I thought you were Brian's girl friend.'

'Hardly.' Jack laughed.

'I know. I mean, when I realized that he – well, it didn't, sort of, match up.'

'It wouldn't.' Jack crossed a leg high on his knee and rearranged his skirt. The biceps of his smooth brown arms – shaved? – looked a bit weird coming out of the sleeveless dress. Above the light scarf which covered his Adam's apple, his throat was as sinewy as you would expect. 'No, Brian and I are friends. I share this house with him because he doesn't mind me cross-dressing. He understands.'

'Understands what?' Tim's mind was seething with questions, none of which he was able to ask.

'About me. Not many people do, Tim. That's why I'm grateful to you for not being shocked.'

I am shocked.

'How do you like the dress? Marks and Sparks. Very useful, they are, because the sizes don't vary.'

138

Jack chatted on, quite casually and naturally, but Tim did not want to hear any more. He finished his coffee and put the mug down in a gesture of departing.

'Just one thing.' Under the golden wig which had been all right when Tim thought it was a woman's hair, but now was grotesque, Jack looked a bit nervous. 'This is between you and me. Nothing said at Webster's.'

'What about' – Tim had to voice the bewilderment – 'what about Janet Fox?'

'She doesn't know, although we're close friends. She's talked about us being married. Bit awkward really.' Jack stretched his half-painted mouth in the shape of a grin, without life to it. 'She'd have to get used to me wearing a nightie in bed.'

A nightie. That did it. Tim had been holding down all the objections of his Wallace Kendall heritage, but they came charging up and delivered the word: disgusting.

He got up, mumbled an excuse and escaped to his eyrie.

Disgusting.

Hang on a minute. What about him in bed with the pistol and the cammo?

'You've got some of our stuff.' Derek rang Tim that evening.

'I'm sending it back. First post tomorrow.'

'Why did we lose you?'

'I had to go. I didn't feel well.'

'Come off it. I heard you ran like hell for the flag.'

'Oh – well, I – yes. Thanks.' Tim managed a short laugh. 'Feverish. Thought I was coming down with something.'

'You sound all right now.'

'Oh. Yes. I'm all right today.'

Well, not as all right as I was before I had that talk with Jack. He's kinky. I'm kinky. The whole world is kinky. 'Five per cent of men in business suits have got women's underwear on underneath,' Jack had said.

Come *on*. Do me a favour.

At work next morning, Tim got some brown paper and tape. He parcelled up the gun wrapped in the cammo overalls with some sadness and a sense of loss, as he saw them go off the post office scales and into the bin behind the counter.

CHAPTER ELEVEN

❧

The relatively normal course of Tim's affairs, which had climaxed with the capture of the flag single-handed and the ravishment of Helen, was only short-lived. Whether the shocking revelation about Jack set it off, or whether it was his biological clock, it was not long before Tim was into one of his far-out phases.

His two weeks' holiday was coming up in September, and he had no idea what he was going to do with it. The Boathouse was closing. He could never do another Enterprise weekend, because of Norman. He could not go back to Warfare, because Derek had sounded stuffy about the overalls and pistol.

If he was a millionaire, he would go to Australia to see Zara, whose last postcard had sounded a bit low, and ended, 'Wish you were here with me.'

His parents had been to the Isle of Wight. The damp had got into his father's chest and they came home two days early. His mother pretended that they had come home because the stairs at the Shanklin Hotel were too much for her. Val and Colin went to the Canaries. Brian climbed a mountain in Scotland with Jack (in camiknickers?). Helen went to stay with her cousin in Hull while Julian was at the camp, also in the Isle of Wight, where he might have come face to face with Wallace Kendall, and spat on his shoe.

Pocket Pickups, chapter 13. 'FOLLOW UP: You're on your way. Follow it up with a bang (excuse pun). Don't give her time to wonder whether to you it was just a one night stand.'

Helen rang up when she got back from Hull. She would have Julian with her now until the end of August. She told Tim that twice, as if to make sure that he got the message, 'Sex is out', not knowing that it was probably good news rather than bad, now that the cammo had gone back to Warfare.

'How is Julian?' Tim wanted to see him. He wanted to feel the strong skinny arms clutching at his neck as the child fought urgently to climb up him, wanted to see the side of the gold-dusted cheek above which the blue eye stared mysteriously beyond him.

'He's fine, I think. I've not heard of any trouble.'

'He'll be glad to get home.'

'Not necessarily. Coming and going is just a part of life to him.'

How do you know? You don't know what goes on inside that princely head. You don't know what goes on inside mine. If you did, you wouldn't ring.

'Well . . .' Helen ended. 'Perhaps we'll see you. Drop in some time.'

'I may do.'

Tim was evasive, because he felt funny, as if his brain were swimming about in a glass jar on a shelf. He got the tape, and measured his small head, to make sure it wasn't shrinking.

Helen did not ring again. Just as well. Lone wolf. He travels fastest who travels alone. Tim bought a pair of black joggers with thick rubber soles and began to prowl when no one was looking, with longer strides and bent knees.

Once, Harold was looking. Tim had gone into the cathedral after a bewildering day at work, to be in a place where people talked quietly, or not at all, and to see if his jangled nerves could find respite in front of the crucifix.

The bench was empty, so he walked twice round the aisles to make it worth sitting down, and paid a visit to the old wall tablet that celebrated Thomas Pargeter, 'whose noble spirit was at last exhausted by the too strenuous endeavours of an urgent mind'.

A nutter, in other words. Takes one to know one.

When he got back to the bench, a woman was sitting there, reading an information pamphlet.

Tim did not want to share that black scarred bench with anyone else. The woman looked up and smiled at him, with teeth bunched forward like a goat. He did not feel like giving out any information, especially as she had the real thing in her hands. He gave the poor man on the cross a glance of same-boat sympathy, and veered away to sit down in a pew in the nave.

A few people were scattered among the pews, one or two genuinely praying, some, like Tim, just part of the furniture. The man who settled with a thump in the pew behind was a heavy breather. He might be having a mystical experience, but he had no right to bother other people with it. Tim slid farther along the pew. At the end, by the central aisle, he gave his head a quarter turn and slid his eyes round to let the man see he was unacceptable, as you did to a driver who passed you at ridiculous speed.

Harold gave him a small salute. When Tim got up, Harold got up too, and caught up with him by the optimistically large contribution box at the bottom of the nave, which was made of glass, so that you could be embarrassed by the smallness of your offering.

'Let's have it, then,' Harold said hoarsely, 'and I'll drop it in there to show how little I care.'

'Drop what?'

'What you owe me.'

'I owe you nothing. Harold' – as the man jostled him – 'not here, for Christ's sake. What's the matter with you? Why don't you leave me alone?'

'I will,' Harold said pulling a toothpick from his pocket and putting it between his teeth, 'when I get my interest.'

'What interest?' Tim would have dodged out, but Harold was in his way, moving with the dexterity of a hod carrier on scaffolding every time Tim moved. 'I paid you your ten per cent.'

'Ten? I said bloody fifteen.'

'*Oh* no.' It was difficult to argue under your breath, and Tim's fear and anger were drawn up and swallowed in the distant immensity of the roof. 'Ten per cent. I wrote it down.'

Harold swung his heavy head from side to side.

'Show me the I O U,' Tim said.

'And let you tear it up?' If Harold's eyes stuck out any farther, they would drop into the collection box. 'Ha! I'm not *stew*-pid.'

No, just bonkers.

'Come outside and let's talk it over,' Tim said despairingly.

'Nothing to talk about.' Harold dusted off his hands.

They went out of the cool grey spaces into the sudden sun. Tim planned to give him the slip among the tombstones and memorials, but Harold walked slowly and deliberately away from him, crunch, crunch on the gravel path, and turned the corner outside the Great Gate of St Bernard, to be swallowed up in the traffic.

Tim prowled about for a while under the yew trees before he went home. This was unbearable. What would come next? Outside the wall of Brian and Jack's house, he looked to see if there was a clod of superhod sitting on the bottom of his steps, or lurking under them, before he went in.

Up in his room, he sat on the window-sill for a long time, and watched the cars, and the late workers walking home. Easy to pick off Harold from here, it would be. He should resurrect the toilet plunger. Or buy a gun.

This was how criminals were made – by lunatics like Harold. Would Tim have to move, to get rid of him? Change his job? Change his name, dye his hair, grow a moustache and beard?

He stayed away from work on Friday, because he was starting the moustache. Over the weekend, Tim constantly fingered his lip and sought counsel with the mirror, and by Monday a light growth of hair was visible.

'What is *that*?' Mr D. pounced immediately at inspection.

'A mus – I'm growing a moustache.'

Lilian sneered. Fred's hands trembled. Gail went off into an explosion of giggles and Mr D. said, 'Go downstairs and buy a disposable razor and dispose of that abomination.'

'Why? I mean, excuse me, but –'

Lilian said, when Mr D. steered his own hairy cow-catcher out of the office to begin his parade up and down among the spotless early-morning cutting tables and the orderly, expectant bolts of cloth, 'You ought to be committed. Only him can have face furniture.'

144

In the staff toilet, Tim said a bitter farewell to his newborn moustache, his disguise, his first step towards a full, ferocious beard that would transform his face into importance.

He went back to the department with clenched fists and a slow tread, fury rising in him like red-hot lava.

'Oh dear,' said Lilian, 'your face looks ever so inflamed.'

So would yours if you had hacked at it savagely with the blade of a plastic razor.

'Still, it's better than that funny fuzz you brought in. I said to Gail, I said, "Look what came out of the carpet sweeper."'

Tim turned away with his shoulders hunched, and paced along the rolls of curtain lining on the back wall. Gorilla man is on the prowl. Hide your babies. The armholes of his suit jacket felt tight and hot. At the rods and fixtures display, he turned to pace back. His friend Mrs Slade was doddering about by the velvets, with a piece of painted wood which she was matching against hopelessly unsuitable colours. As Tim started towards her, Lilian pushed bossily in front of him, rubbing her hands with her elbows out.

'Can I help you?'

Mrs Slade turned her vague face. Tim caught Lilian's stuck-out elbow, heard himself cry, 'I'll kill you!', spun her round and slapped her on the jaw, with a shock of joy from the palm of his hand to his soul.

If Mrs Slade had not tried to bolt, Lilian would not have reeled against her. The old lady staggered, still holding out the piece of wood with the paint sample on it, into a hanging stand of bedroom curtains, and went down among their flowery folds.

For a few days, Tim went off every morning in the dark suit, as if he were going to work. It was quite a relief when Jack found out that he had left Webster's: 'Resigned', which was a dignified translation of 'Got out before he was sacked'.

But it was boring, depressing, degrading. No identity. A nobody. There had been many times when Tim would have given anything not to have to spend all day in the store, but now that he couldn't, he had nothing to do in its place except grow the moustache, and soon nothing much to do the nothing with, as his savings dwindled and his job applications disappeared without trace. He had his phone disconnected. He could not run the car.

Soon, he did not have the car anyway, because Zara came home.

Zara had hoped to stay longer in Australia, but, without a work permit, she had never been able to do more than be a baby-sitter or a cleaner, or a waitress in fringe bars where she fell in with the seductively wrong sort of people from whom she was trying to escape.

Her father was triumphant, since he had known no good would come of Australia. Her mother was happy, because she did not realize Zara was not going to stay at home. Tim fell on his sister with a clutching desperation, as if in his whole life she was the only thing that was stable: a word not normally applied to her.

She could see that he was in one of his rickety phases, poor little Timmy, clinging to reality by the skin of his teeth.

'What's wrong?' she asked him, quite soon after the first excited greetings.

'Nothing, don't be silly. I'm fine. Never better. Freed from the slavery of Mr D.' The unsteady mouth grinned without the eyes, like a marionette.

'What are you going to do now?'

'Oh – lots of offers, you know. Lots of – a lot of things in the fire.'

Val would have retorted, 'Such as?' to a flight of fancy like that. Zara, wary of jolting Tim down to earth, as if he were a sleepwalker, said, 'That's fine.'

'Everything's fine now you're here.'

Zara said cautiously, 'Remember, you haven't got to pretend with me, darling.'

'Oh, I'm not, I'm not, why would I do that? It's like, it's –
everything's going great.'

He had that slightly feverish look, nervous brown eyes not quite
meeting yours. Watching him, she saw that he blinked a lot, and
had developed a little twitch in the hollow under one cheek. He
was biting his nails again, which he had stopped doing when his
hands were on show at the fabric counter.

Their mother wanted a big family Sunday lunch, with a turkey.
'Why do I dream of turkey, although it's not Christmas?'

'Because it's cheaper at this time of year,' Wally said.

Tim told Zara he didn't want to come.

'Because of Wally?'

'I don't want him banging on about me being unem – not at Webster's.'

'But he was always down on the shop when you were there.'

'He'll change his tune when I start one of these better jobs I've
been interviewed for.'

'So, up *his*,' Zara said. 'Come for the food, if not for me.'

She had taken Tim out for a couple of meals, and tried to eat the
carbohydrates which helped her to keep down on the booze. Her
little Timmy was as ravenous as he had been as a teenager.

❧

On Sunday morning, Tim lost his nerve and shaved off the seedling
moustache, but Little Hitler could not have been fouler about
Webster's, so he might as well have kept it.

'I hate him.' Tim went into the kitchen and clenched his fists at
his mother.

'No, Tim, no, you don't.' Annie lifted saucepan lids and steamed
her rosy face.

'You know what he said to me? He said, when I told him I'd
been treated like dirt for doing abso – absolutely nothing, he said,
"Looks as if they were waiting for a chance to get rid of you."'

'Don't pay any attention to him, love. He's not very well.'

147

'He's been pulling that one ever since I can remember.'

'I'll tell you what it is,' Tim's mother said with surprising honesty. 'He was never liked at work, you know, so he didn't want *you* to be.'

After lunch, Tim, Zara, Val and Colin sat in the garden and planned how to set fire to the workshop shed – with Little Hitler in it.

'How's Helen?' Valerie asked Tim.

'Oh – I don't know. O K, I suppose. Haven't seen her.'

'Oh?' Val said, in that swooping voice of disbelief. 'Well, not much loss, I suppose. Now let's hope you can find someone your own age, who doesn't look like the back end of a bus going north.'

Tim – wake up! Stand up for Helen. Be a knight – throw down the gauntlet, whatever it is they do – don't let her jeer at Helen like that.

'Shut – shut up,' was all he could say. 'You introduced us.'

'Last hopes.'

Valerie's laugh made even Colin raise the black loops of his eyebrows and say mildly, 'Valerie . . .'

'Trouble with you,' Val kept on at Tim, 'you don't meet people.'

'How do you know?'

'You don't *go* anywhere or *do* anything.'

'I do!'

He was goaded to tell them about Enterprise and about Warfare, exaggerating as much as he thought he could get away with. When he told the truth, no one believed it. They never had. As a child, it had not been worth not lying.

'In three of the battles, I was the one who ran for the flag. They're sniping at you from all round see, and you got to kill 'em off and grab their flag and –'

'Why?' Val, short and sharp.

'Why grab the flag?'

'No, moron. Why did you want to play that kind of pseudo-macho nonsense?'

'It was fun,' Tim said stubbornly.

'*I* bet.' Colin was giving him a calculating look.

'I was good at it. I – I excelled.'

'So would Barry McCarthy, if he had played it,' Colin said. 'I'd keep quiet about that weekend, Timothy, if I were you. After a massacre like Green Ponds, people begin to watch the loners.'

'Colin, friend, sometimes my feeling is that you go a little bit too far.'

If anyone was going to insult her brother, Val could do it herself.

Zara, who had been asleep on the grass, woke up to see Tim jerk clumsily out of his chair and lurch into the house.

'What have you been saying to my little Timmy?'

'He's in bad shape,' Val said in her psychological voice. 'He's got real problems.'

'Who wouldn't, in this family?'

'He needs some first-class counselling.' Val and Colin both nodded sagely, as if they were prepared to take on the job.

'He needs love,' Zara said.

She took Tim out for a drink before he went home. He wanted a second, so Zara had to have one with him, and then another, because quite suddenly, while they were dreaming fantastic schemes about living and working together, he started to weep, in a back booth at the Stag.

Zara did not know what she was going to do. It was all she could do to cope with herself. How was she going to cope with Timmy?

CHAPTER TWELVE

❧

He would join a cult. He would live like a tribal man, guided, sheltered, exploited, brainwashed. Might be worth it. This poor old brain could do with a wash.

He would become a monk. He would join the Army and send Sergeant Joe a postcard: 'Wish you were here.' He would go down the mines, pack fish in a Grimsby freezing plant, march with a demo, join a riot, anywhere, for any cause.

Term had started at the Hall School again. Tim went down there one afternoon, and saw Helen shepherding children over the street crossing, with the absurd pole and lollipop sign, which wouldn't stop a bicycle, let alone a car, the way some maniacs drove in this town.

Since he had lost Buttercup, Tim had switched sides again in the pedestrian–driver conflict.

Helen was wearing a green fluorescent vest back and front, and the high-peaked cap that made her face severe. When the parents and the children thinned out, Tim went over to her.

'Studying my style?' She lowered the top of the pole to the ground, like a lance. 'You must be hard up for something to do.'

'I am.' Tim wanted to put his arms round the lime green vest and kiss her under the harsh peak of the hat, which might have excited the mothers and children, if not Helen. 'Left my job.'

'Oh, Tim, I *am* sorry.'

'I'm not. I was sick of it.'

She left him, to beckon across some older children.

'What happened?' she asked when she came back.

'Slight difference of opinion. Can't tell you now.'

'No, of course not.' She looked into his face, and what she saw made her say, 'Come to my place, can you? Will you come back with me now?'

'I'd rather come on Saturday – when Julian's there.'

'Well!' She made a surprised face. 'That's nice of you. We'll both like that.'

When Tim went to Helen's flat, he did not want to talk about Webster's. How could he explain it to her? By now, fact and myth had become so interwoven that he was not sure exactly what had happened.

After Helen opened the door, Julian refused to walk back up-stairs, but he allowed Tim to carry him without making a fuss. This felt to Tim as great an achievement as if the boy had said, 'Hello, Timothy Kendall, how are you?'

When he put him down, Julian made one of his dancing runs over to the bottom shelf, and pulled out some tattered books, casting them over the floor as if he were sowing seed. Tim sat down and pulled the child towards him.

'I'll read to you.' He picked up a book and started to read the babyish words, but Julian flipped over the pages, and then threw the book away and went to the corner to turn his basket of toys upside-down. He sat with the empty basket over his head, sending out a monotonous chant through the plastic slats.

'Come and sit on the sofa, Tim,' Helen said. 'Tell me about the job. I thought you wanted to make a career in retailing.'

'There's other things in life. Time to make a change.'

'Why? Did something – Julian!' She dived across the room, as Julian, still wearing the basket, lifted the big coloured top above his head to hurl it at the window. She fetched his soapy sponge, and left him lathering his arms and his naked stomach under the shirt that was hanging round his neck.

When she came back to Tim, she knelt down in front of the sofa and leaned on his knees.

'Tell me,' she said. 'Did you leave, or did they sack you?' It was not coaxing or sympathetic, just a practical request for information.

Tim put a hand on her dry oatmeal hair. 'Are you still my oppo?' He had called her that in bed.

'If you want. Tell me what happened.'

He sighed. 'I clobbered Lilian.' He had not told anybody that, although he thought that Jack might know, from store gossip.

'Oh well,' Helen said briskly, and got up. 'I daresay she asked for it.'

Dribbling and waving his arms, Julian came over to Tim and climbed painfully on to his lap, kicking his shin with his shoes. He leaned against Tim's chest, breathing heavily, forced open his lips and tried to pull out his teeth. When Tim pretended to bite, Julian screamed and clutched a handful of Tim's hair, jerking his head sideways. Tim screamed too.

'Here.' Helen put down plates with slices of cake. 'This should keep you both quiet. He usually behaves better at the table. The school's strict about that.'

Julian would not touch the cake until Helen had also put down a banana which he moved to a certain precise spot, touching it again and again until he was satisfied it was exactly right.

He grabbed for Tim's cup of tea, and Helen said sternly, 'No. If you want a drink, you must ask for it.'

'How, if he doesn't talk?'

'Talk,' Julian echoed obediently.

'At school, they teach them signs for things like please and thank you, and I'm supposed to make him use them. Drink.' She raised a cupped hand to her mouth. 'Julian – look. Drink.' The child kept on grabbing and whining.

Feeling self-conscious, Tim made the 'drink' gesture. He and Helen must have looked like a couple of pantomime fools.

'He'll never sign for me,' Helen said. 'I'm a failure. Shall I give him his tea anyway?'

'Yes.' Tim felt in control. 'Look, Prince Julian,' he said. 'I brought a picture for you.'

It was a magazine colour photograph of a swan reflected in a lake, steering a gliding course among flowing white water lilies.

Tim had taken an old photograph out of its frame, and fitted the swan picture into it. He held it up, moving it as Julian moved his eyes sideways away from it. 'It's yours.' He put it on the table.

'Make the sign for thank you,' Helen said hopefully.

'Listen.' Tim sat opposite the beautiful boy, who was picking his piece of cake into its component parts of raisins and cherries and crumbs. 'I'll tell you a story.' He looked fixedly at Julian, as he had looked at Norman to hypnotize him, and pretended that Julian was looking at him.

'There was this prince, you see . . .'

On the journey to Helen's flat, with its irritating wait and change of buses, he had thought about the legend of the Sleeping Beauty, and the kiss that broke the spell.

'This prince, he'd, like, been asleep for a hundred years. Lovely dreams, he had, of rivers and swans, and about how one day he would be a king with his own golden boat, and be the most clever and important and best-loved person in the whole land.'

The dreams were Tim's. He could see them pass behind his eyes. What hidden dreams flickered behind the child's averted eyes?

'They wanted him to wake up and be the king, only nobody could budge him. Want to know how they got him to wake up in the end?'

Julian pressed his wet finger on to the last crumb of cake, then hammered the edge of the plate on to the swan picture, breaking the glass.

Tim did not know whether Helen wanted to go to bed with him again or not. She did not say anything about meeting during the week when Julian was away at school, so Tim did not suggest it. He did not think his wobbly confidence could stand up to hearing her say no.

Quite suddenly, Tim's father became ill. He was in a bed in the hospital, and the doctor told Annie that it might be lung cancer and that he needed an operation.

'Does he know, Mum?'

'No, dear. Better he doesn't.'

But was it better to rob Little Hitler of the triumph of knowing that he was right and they were wrong about his chest?

Tim went to the hospital with his mother. He did not want to go alone, and have nothing to say.

'Shall I pretend I've found a job?' he asked his mother, while they were waiting outside the ward for visiting time to start.

She smiled. 'It would please him.' (Tim had thought of it as a defence, not an offering.) 'What shall it be, then? Computer firm, local paper, school caretaker, secretary to a rich old lady?' Annie plunged into the game. 'No.' She dropped her smile. 'He's very ill, but I'm afraid he'd still see through you.'

Tim was at 23 The Avenue with his mother and Sarah (she had gone back to that name when she started drinking again), when the hospital rang to say that his father had not survived the operation.

Tim stayed the night in his old room with the spooky trap door, while Sarah slept in the big Hitler bed with their mother. In the kitchen next morning, Sarah, looking ghastly, as she did these days without make-up, said, through her first cigarette, 'How awful to die being someone that nobody liked.'

'Mum liked him.'

'Do her a favour.' Sarah pushed back her sleep-tangled hair. 'She's got better taste than that.'

Tim got home to find one of Harold's little cards on the mat. 'I got my i on U,' and a crude drawing of an eye.

Leave me alone. Tim threw the card into the waste-bin. I'm busy. I'm upset.

He was surprised by the effect of his father's death. He felt absolutely rotten for a few days. Now that it was too late, he liked his father better, and the sadness was for all the wasted time when they might have been friends. He unlocked Wallace's workshop, and helped himself to a couple of the small woodworking tools, which were to be sold as a set, and put them criss-cross on the shelf over his bed at the flat. He began to build a little fantasy around the phantom of Wallace Kendall as a dependable father-figure, and himself as a deprived and grieving orphan.

❧

Brian and Jack sent Tim a sympathy card. 'Through the post,' Jack said, 'will look more sincere than me just carrying it upstairs and shoving it through the slot.'

'Especially dressed like that.'

'He wouldn't mind. Actually, he's seen me cross-dressed.'

'Oh, look, the boy's as mad as a hatter already,' Brian said. 'Do you want to send him completely round the bend?'

'Reality never hurt anyone.'

'How did he take it?' Brian asked, with a curious delight.

'Like a man.'

❧

The grieving orphan was surprised by a belated answer to a job application, asking him to turn up for an interview at a fabric shop in Walker's Piece, the pedestrian precinct that joined two of the town's main streets.

It was his first offer of an interview. Why wasn't he jumping at the chance? Because I'm bereaved, he was able to tell himself, to disguise the truth that he was scared. Getting no answers to applications was damaging enough. Failing at an interview would undo him.

For the decision, he turned once again to his oracle, the dictionary. The shop was called Sew What, so he opened the book at *se*, closed his eyes and let his finger fall on 'seal'. Your fate is sealed, quoth the oracle.

Yes, but which way? He tried *j* for 'job', and got 'joyous'. Too good to be true. Just to make sure, he opened the book at *f* for 'fabric'. His finger fell on 'foothold'. His fate *was* sealed. He was about to get a foothold in the world of commerce again.

155

The manageress of Sew What was brisk and spiky, with close-cut black hair decorated with a silver streak from brow to crown. The shop sold dress and curtain fabrics, and also patterns and dressmaking accessories of all kinds.

'As an assistant, you would have to be familiar with all those lines.' Mrs Barber eyed Tim narrowly.

'Oh, I – I am.' He could learn them up.

'What's this, then, Mr Kendall?' She held out a small instrument with a spiked wheel, that looked like the gadget his mother used to cut pastry.

He could not say, 'My mother's pastry cutter,' so he said, 'You got me there,' with a wide-open smile to disarm her.

After warning him that the first person who had been hired for the job had lost it in a week for slack practices, she sent him away, with no sign in her face or voice of what his chances were.

Nil. She might as well have said it then and there, instead of, 'We'll let you know.'

Save the stamp. Depressed, Tim walked slowly past the narrow shop front to assure himself that the pitiful display of fanned-out fabric lengths could not be mentioned in the same breath as Webster's windows.

The letter from Sew What told him to turn up for work the following Monday. He took the dark suit to his mother to be sponged and pressed. She was doing well, her usual optimistic self, but she remembered to bring her husband into the conversation from time to time.

'Your father would be proud of you,' she told Tim.

'Yeah, he would.'

They both believed that it was true.

Mrs Barber, the hedgehog manager – all smooth and serene one minute, and prickles up the next – told Tim that he had got a fair reference from Webster's. 'The termination of his employment was mutual,' they had written (God bless them). 'An enthusiastic worker, but a bit of a dreamer.'

'What does that mean, I wonder, Mr Kendall?'

It did not look as if she would ever call him Timothy or Tim.

'I couldn't say.'

'Does it mean you are vague and lazy?'

'No, it – it means – er, creative. That's it. An idealist.'

Compared to the lost splendours of Webster's huge Fabric and Soft Furnishings, Sew What was nothing to write home about. The shop was long and narrow, like a coffin, and some of the goods, and the customers who looked, fingered, bought or did not buy, Webster's would not have been seen dead with.

A lot of the colours and patterns were very harsh. 'Modern,' Mrs Barber called them. 'This is a very modern design, madam,' to an old lady with a leather shopping-bag on wheels who was giving the suspicious finger to a zigzag of black and white stripes with silver threads.

Tim's special hates were the hideous rolls of ugliness called waterproof tabletop vinyl, disfigured with patterns of ladies in violet crinolines and sunshades, and bright pink gambolling babies.

Heaving the roll of naked babies back on the stand after a moronic mother had parted with three pound twenty for a metre and a half, Tim could not help reminiscing about the fabulous goods he had handled at Webster's. 'The velvets alone, Mrs Barber, were like a fairy-tale.'

'Don't chatter.' Mrs Barber was not impressed. 'Keep quiet, Mr Kendall, and sell the tabletop vinyl.'

When Tim got his first money, he paid off some of his back rent, and rang Helen from a phone-box to tell her about the job. They arranged to meet in a café after he got out of work.

Helen had got a new wool tunic for the autumn. It was oatmeal – how she loved those non-colours – and hung straight down in a way that improved her waist and hips.

'What do you think about coming back to my place?' Tim had rehearsed all afternoon how he would say that. He had not minded a long, argumentative session with a bullying customer who wanted to exchange a length of material into which she had already put pin marks, followed by a stiff session explaining it to Mrs Barber when she came back from lunch, because he was going to say to Helen, 'What do you think about coming back to my place?'

Inside the flat, she saw the woodworking tools displayed, in memoriam, over the couch.

'My Dad died.'

'Oh, Tim, I am sorry. You must miss him.'

'Oh, I do. I've been quite cut up.'

'Poor Tim.'

They sat on the couch and she kissed him gently, and put her short soft arms round him in a comfortable, motherly way. They lay down together, but she was still being soothing and motherly, and that would not do now.

'Helen, I' – if only you could just *do* sex, and never have to talk about it – 'it won't work this way.'

'What way, then?'

'I, you know, need to be – well, not like a kid, but – well, remember the cammo? Like, the master.'

'Oh, so you do, that's right. What shall we do, then?'

'I'll be the man coming home from work, or a war, or something.'

Tim got up and went to the door, but did not go out and come in again, in case anyone might see from downstairs. He wiped his feet on the rubber mat tyrannically, like a dog after it has peed. Helen was standing up, smiling, with clasped hands. She had put on Tim's frying apron, to look submissive.

The conversation went something like, 'On the bed, woman!'

'Oh, goodness.'

He stripped off the apron, pushed her down on the bed, and stripped off a few other things. She giggled and said, 'Ooh,' and he growled a war lord's growl, and took a few nips at her.

Afterwards, Tim took Helen home, because it was getting dark, and because he wanted to, although she had said, 'I can look after myself.'

When she asked, 'Why don't you come upstairs?', Tim said,

'You don't have to ask me, if you – I mean, I don't want you to think –'

'Oh, I don't.'

What didn't he want her to think?

Helen's bed was wider than Tim's couch, and softer. They both disappeared into the middle of it, and sank through into the place where words did not matter any more.

Chapter Thirteen

❧

One slack day when only Tim and Mrs Barber were in the shop, he put some dress patterns away into the bottom drawer, and stood up to look through the window straight into the bulging eyes of Harold Trotman.

Tim retreated, as Harold burst through the glass door with a roar and came at him, knocking over everything in his path. The big cutting scissors were on the counter. Harold seized them and raised them high, like a dagger.

'Oh, give me those, you stupid man.' Mrs Barber grabbed his arm with both hands, but Harold shook her off, and she gave a gasp, and brought her hands away, bleeding.

Tim had backed against the shelves, but when he saw the blood, he picked up the nearest bolt of cloth and, using it as a battering ram, charged into the great expanse of Harold's stomach, hanging over his belt.

The scissors fell to the floor against Tim's foot. The howls and gurgles of the toppling giant were like Wurmagh the terrible sea python, pierced in the livid underbelly by the halberd-carrying figurehead of Varth's brigantine. Harold went down, winded, and Tim held him pinned by the neck under the heavy roll of tabletop vinyl, with the naked pink babies.

That was how the police found them: Tim kneeling on the heaving stomach of Harold, who stared at the ceiling as if it were a horror film, snoring strangled breaths through his furred snout, the two ginger hairs in the middle of his nose waving for help.

Mrs Barber, her hand wrapped in a piece of bloody seersucker from the remnant bin, did not scold Tim for having such undesirable friends. She thanked him, and told the police, 'This young man saved me.'

'It was nothing.' Tim sat down on the floor to take off his shoe and sock and inspect the small cut where the scissors had nicked his ankle. And to keep his head down, to hide the glow.

He had rescued a maiden – at last, at last! No matter that it was only Mrs Barber.

Tim was a local hero. The story was in the papers, with a picture of him, holding the roll of tabletop vinyl and grinning like a hobgoblin.

'Local man defeats attacker. "I'm proud of him," Walker's Piece manager says.'

The police had praised him, right there in the shop, in front of the small crowd of sightseers who had materialized from nowhere in the empty precinct.

After Harold had been trundled away, the one who was in charge said, 'The Chief Constable may want to talk to you.'

'As long as you didn't dweam this up too,' the other one said, and winked. It was Constable Somebody, who couldn't pronounce his *r*'s.

Tim's family were hugely proud. His mother became famous in the neighbourhood. Sarah wept a tear or two over her little Timmy, who might have been killed. Even Valerie told him, 'I don't care what anyone says. You did the right thing.'

Tim felt as if all the mistakes of his dodgy past life had been washed away, and he had come into his own, like a conqueror.

Valiant Varth, mighty Warlord Blch, imperishable Tohubo – the victory is ours!

'We knew it all along,' Jack and Brian told Tim. 'We knew you had it in you.'

'Oh – it was nothing.'

'We're going to nominate you for the Queen's commendation for bravery,' Brian said. 'Our tenant, our good old boy.'

More people came into the shop, to stare, and ask questions, and look to see if there was any blood on the floor, but after a while, things were back to normal. Harold had appeared briefly in the magistrate's court, and been remanded for 'social and psychiatric reports'. That should make hot reading.

Sarah had left 23 The Avenue and moved back in with the man from Barbados who was one of the reasons she had run away to Australia. Tim was troubled by the guilty feeling that he ought to go and live with his mother.

'I could take care of you, Mum. Look after the place, keep you company.'

'And I would cook you wonderful meals, keep your clothes nice, play cards like we used to. We could re-decorate your old room . . .'

'I'll paint the kitchen for you.'

'We'll have parties.'

'I'll buy you a pretty dress.'

' "Tim and Annie," they'll say, "Aren't they a pair?" '

'Take you on a cruise.'

'Never a cross word.'

'Mum.' Tim suddenly plummeted down. 'It wouldn't be like that.'

'I know.' She followed him down at once. 'I couldn't let you live here with me anyway. Too big a burden for you.'

'No, that's all right, really.' Here came guilt again. 'I'd like it.' Sacrifice his freedom. The hero with a heart of gold.

'Too late.' His mother told him that she had already decided to sell the inconvenient house and live in a flat.

'Well, don't worry. I'll come round a lot.'

'I hope so. I'll need someone to cook for.'

'I mean, to do odd jobs and that. When I get my own car, I'll take you out.'

'We'll go to the sea. Could we go to Scotland? Your Dad would never go over the border.'

'Go anywhere you like. Isle of Skye . . . West End theatres . . .'

They were off again, painting pictures in which they did not have to believe.

'I love you, son,' she told him when he left.

Helen gave him quiet praise for his great feat, in a few short rushes of words. Then she changed the subject, which he liked, because you couldn't go on and on about it for ever.

'What can I give you, brave Tim? I want to give you a treat.'

'Let me come with you when you go to Julian's school next week.'

He wanted to see the boy. In his new disguise as hero, he wanted to lay his deed at the feet of the prince, as if the boy could enter into the legend, and knight him Sir Galahad.

'But it's a Wednesday.'

'I'll get the afternoon off.'

Mrs Barber was not exactly putty in his hands, but she was a lot less sharp and spiky.

There were about twenty children at the school, all of them autistic. Tim and Helen found them at dinner, bigger boys crouched or sprawled over a normal-sized table by the wall, the smaller ones at low tables and chairs.

Helen saw Julian at once, but it took Tim a moment to recognize his arrogant rebel prince. He was sitting so quietly at the corner of the table, one hand combing his hair with a knife, the other eating mashed potato with a fork, which he never did at home. Mashed potato was for the hands.

Helen took Tim over to sit at Julian's table.

'All right?'

Tim nodded and smiled at her, as if he were comfortable on the low chair; but he was as embarrassed as if everyone were looking at him, which no one was, because autistic children don't look at people, and the staff were busy helping, correcting, feeding small children who opened their mouths like baby birds, then jerked their heads away, and chatting cheerfully to children who did not answer.

Someone was looking at Tim. A pale girl with a drooping mouth, the ends of her long hair wound round her neck like a scarf, was staring through him with mournful grey eyes. Unexpectedly, she clapped her hands and whistled.

'Eat your dinner, Megan.'

She clapped again, then screwed her eyes shut, crumpled her chalky face into a crying shape, dumped her head into her plate, and put her hands on the back of it to cover her ears.

The middle-aged woman at the table pulled the plate out from under her face, but left her alone.

'It's not you.' She smiled at Tim. She had two homely brown moles on one cheek. 'She does that to shut out everything, when she can't deal with something new.'

Julian scrambled up and knocked over his chair.

'Pick it up,' said the bearded young man next to him. Some hope, mate. But the child did pick it up. 'If you want to get up, Julian, what do you say?'

The wilful boy, Tim's untamed wild boy, put up a hand and patted his mouth for 'please'.

'What do you want?'

Helen watched with her deep frown, as Julian lifted a cupped hand to his mouth.

'Go ahead.'

Julian went to the serving hatch for a glass of water.

'I'm ashamed,' Helen said. 'It's very humiliating. I can't get him to do any of those things at home.'

'That's why he's here,' the teacher said. 'And I bet you feel guilty about that too.'

'How did you know?'

'All the parents do. But you'd feel guiltier struggling to cope with him all the time at home, and failing, and going bonkers.'

Julian came back with the water.

'Sit down, Julian.'

He sat. He drank some water, and then began to lick all round outside the plastic glass. He spilled a drop and licked it off the table, again and again. Spill a drop, bend, lick it up, spill a drop more. He was busy, and unnaturally peaceful. It was almost a relief when he suddenly hurled the glass across the table, and screamed and threw himself about, and had to be restrained by Helen and the imperturbable young man. Tim sat like a bump on a log, and the pale sad girl kept her head down on the table, with her hands over her ears.

Out in the playground, one of the teenagers went off to sit on a tree stump in a hedge, another did a silly walk on the tips of his toes, and another big boy took a small tricycle away from a little one, and rode it round and round, with his jacket on backwards and his knees up to his chin.

The bigger ones were more distressing. Helen worried, 'What shall I do when Julian is that size?'

Tim shook his head. He had got used to being with the one strange little tyrant. Seeing this assorted group, each one self-absorbed, ignoring the others, except to hit out at random, baffled him into silence.

A stout girl with a fixed grin kept up a monotonous chant. 'Where's Angela why's Angela where's Angela.' She laughed at nothing, and droned, 'Lo house lo trees lo person lo Simon. All right, Simon? Lo Simon all right?'

'All right, thanks,' the unruffled young man answered, ten, twenty, thirty times, as many as was necessary.

The sad girl was lying inside a big plastic play tube, like a sewer pipe, with the hood of her jacket pulled down over her face and her hands over her ears, rolling from side to side.

When Helen sat down on a bench, Julian came and climbed on to her lap. Tim sat down, but Julian would not come to him. This was disappointing. Tim wanted to impress the staff.

Oh, you're so good with the boy, a real natural. Ever thought about going in for this kind of work? Tim the teacher. Loved and trusted. He could have another go at that moustache and beard.

Julian ignored him completely, would not climb up, jabber and dribble over him, try to pull out his teeth and hair. Tim felt low. He felt out of it and useless.

He felt better when the teacher with the moles knew who he was.

'I recognized you from your picture in the papers. Took the law into your own hands, didn't you? We need more of that. Listen, Julian.' She stood the boy in front of her and knelt on the damp playground to look into his angelic, uncaring face. 'This is your friend Timothy and he was very brave. He's come to see you. *You*. Because he's your friend and he's a brave man, and he loves you. Right, Timothy?'

'Right.' Tim's heart lifted with pride. He galloped out at the head of a posse of vigilantes, mowing down the muggers and scum.

'Right, Julian?'

The boy pulled away from her – he could be amazingly strong, and slippery – and ran behind the playhouse in the far corner, hitting out at a smaller child who ambled into his path without looking at him.

'He doesn't understand,' Tim said glumly.

The teacher got up and brushed off her sensible tan trousers. 'But it may get through. Like talking to someone under an anaesthetic. You never know. And he understands love. They all do.'

Everyone was called inside. The big boy on the tree stump stood up, turned round, and bent to smooth and pat the stump, as if it were a sofa cushion. He came out of the hedge, then went back and made the identical movements with his hands, left the hedge, went back again, like a woman compulsively checking her stove.

Julian was the last to go in. He waited behind the playhouse, then made a dash for a corner of the building, where he clung on to a drainpipe, licking it, until he was taken inside.

'We'd better go,' Helen said to Tim. 'I hope you – oh well. I'm sorry.'

'What about?'

'You know. He usually behaves better here, and I begin to think he's improving. Then I think he's not.'

She looked tired, and bitter. Tim could have taken her hand or her arm, but there were people about in the hall. They went towards the door, and were saying goodbye to Simon, when the amazing thing happened.

They saw Julian streak into the hall from somewhere, and zigzag between grown-ups and children to the far wall where pictures were pinned up. He pulled a small picture roughly down, and streaked back to the door, put the picture in Tim's hand, and walked away without looking at him.

It was a torn, scribbled-over picture of a swan cruising out of a clump of reeds.

'He tore it out of a book,' Simon said. 'He insisted on having it put up on the wall. Does it mean something special?'

Earlier, in the playground, Simon had told them that it had taken him two and a half years to teach one boy of fourteen to dress himself, and added, 'I was as pleased as if I'd taught a three-year-old to do it in one day.'

You're easy to please, mate, Tim had thought. Now he understood.

On his next free Saturday, Tim turned up at Helen's flat. She had nothing for their supper, so she asked Tim to go out. 'I can't face taking Julian.'

'You go,' Tim said. 'I'll stay with him.'

'Are you sure?'

'Nothing to it.' Tim wanted to try some of the things he had seen at the school.

After Helen left, Julian was scudding about like a crazed beetle. Tim caught and held him, and went down on his knees like the woman teacher, and talked into his face.

'I'm your friend,' he said. 'Your friend, Tim. I'm going to tell you a story.'

When Helen was there, he supposed he was talking half to her. Now it felt odd to be speaking into a vacuum, but there was one thing about a boy like this. You didn't have to feel shy, since he did not take any notice of you.

'Let's sit on the floor and I'll tell you some more about the sleeping prince. Here, I'll build you a castle.'

Chattering away in a moronic manner that surprised himself, Tim began to pile up light plastic blocks to make a castle keep. A piece of cardboard was the drawbridge, with Helen's knitting wool (kept on top of the cupboard) to pull it up.

'This is a castle. It's ours. We're going to live in it. And have swans on the moat.' Tim made a long, curving-neck gesture with his hands. 'Here – do like this. *Swans*, Julian. Swans.' That was the simple, patient way they talked to the children at the school.

While Tim added to his castle, Julian wandered out of the room. 'If he's quiet, go and see what he's doing,' Helen had said.

He had done it. He had messed himself, and the bottom of his bedroom door. Tim ran a shallow bath, and dumped him into it. Although Julian struggled, once he was in the water, it was impossible to get him to come out. He fought to stay with the plastic toys and wooden spoons, but Tim wanted him to be dried and dressed before Helen came home.

Julian would not leave the bath, so Tim pulled up the plug and let the water out. Screams and gnashing of teeth, and a struggle to stop him getting to the tap to turn the water on again. Tim wrapped him in a ragged towel – all the towels and teacloths were bitten and torn – and carried him to the sofa.

For a moment, Julian let Tim hold him in the towel, clean and flushed, with damp golden curls. Then he was off and gone, naked and long-legged.

Tim folded the towel and went to find clean clothes. While he was at the laundry basket in the kitchen, flushing sounds were coming from the bathroom. Helen had said, 'Don't forget to keep the bathroom door locked. He puts in the basin plug and holds his hands on the overflow, and the people downstairs get a waterfall through their ceiling.'

She did not say that Julian would also put the end of the toilet roll into the pan, and flush and flush, as the paper unrolled down the pipe.

He had already stopped it up. Where's my doughty sniper's rifle/toilet plunger? Better get him dressed first. How does she *do* this four or five times a day? 'Hold still, you little bugger.' Tim got trousers and a vest on him, and was exhausted.

Julian climbed on to a chair at the table, and screeched like an owl.

'What do you say?' Tim put his hand to his own mouth, in the 'please' sign.

Julian did nothing, but Tim gave him a mug of milk anyway, and a biscuit. Pandemonium. Chaos. Wrong mug. Wrong kind of biscuit. No banana. Banana in wrong place.

'If you're clever enough to know what you want, you're clever enough to behave,' Tim said, not tolerantly, like Simon, but with a rather hysterical severity.

Julian looked at him. *He looked at him.* He was so beautiful. Tim bent down and kissed him on the perfect curve at the side of his mouth.

'Have you killed each other?' Helen came in with her shopping-bag. Julian slid under the table.

'He's been fine.'

'That's why you gave him a bath and changed his clothes.'

'We managed all right. Have you got a toilet plunger?'

Later, Tim sat on the child's bed and finished the story of the kiss that woke the sleeping prince, and what happened after he had been asleep for a hundred years.

Silver-tongued, he sat by the great hearth at the inn, firelight and shadows playing on his strong, wise face. Blch, the lone wandering minstrel, teller of tales. Julian could not follow him. The warlord's faithful followers were lost, trapped in the stark tundra.

He travels fastest . . .

But you've got to have someone to tell the tales to.

'Helen,' Tim called to her. 'Are you divorced?'

'No, just separated.'

'Well, we wouldn't have to be married.'

'What do you mean?' she called from the other room. 'Live to-gether?'

'We might do.'

Julian picked busily at pills of wool on Tim's green sweater, a monkey grooming a monkey. It occurred to Tim: I have never really loved anyone before.

When Tim cleared out his things, his plain girl friend came too, with a handicapped child in tow, who fell off the top of the outside stairs, but bounced.

'It shouldn't be hard to get another tenant,' Brian said when they had gone.

'I'll get Janet to put a notice up in the main office.'

'We can raise the rent now.'

'I'll miss old Tim, though.' Cindy was in a kimono, painting her nails, although the polish would have to come off before Jack went to work on Monday. 'Do you think it will last?'

'It's so bizarre, it just might,' Brian said.

'Wouldn't you think she had enough, with one nutty kid, without taking on another?'

'She collects them.'

'I've sometimes thought I'd like to do that, Bri, if you're not going to give me a child . . .'